Also by R. Anton Hough

Halcyon Fury

NO SWIMMING

R. ANTON HOUGH

*To Sheri
with very best
wishes
Tony Hough*

∞ INFINITY
PUBLISHING

All rights reserved. No part of this book shall be reproduced or transmitted in any form or by any means, electronic, mechanical, magnetic, photographic including photocopying, recording or by any information storage and retrieval system, without prior written permission of the publisher. No patent liability is assumed with respect to the use of the information contained herein. Although every precaution has been taken in the preparation of this book, the publisher and author assume no responsibility for errors or omissions. Neither is any liability assumed for damages resulting from the use of the information contained herein.

Copyright © 2013 by R. Anton Hough
Cover photograph by Victoria Brueckmann Hough
Author photograph by Victoria Brueckmann Hough

ISBN 978-0-7414-8276-1 Paperback
ISBN 978-0-7414-8277-8 eBook
Library of Congress Control Number: 2013901105

Printed in the United States of America

This is a work of fiction. Names, characters, places, and incidents either are the product of the author's imagination or are used fictitiously. Any resemblance to actual events or locales or persons, living or dead, is entirely coincidental.

Published March 2013

INFINITY PUBLISHING
1094 New DeHaven Street, Suite 100
West Conshohocken, PA 19428-2713
Toll-free (877) BUY BOOK
Local Phone (610) 941-9999
Fax (610) 941-9959
Info@buybooksontheweb.com
www.buybooksontheweb.com

For Lynn

Prologue

The noonday Caribbean sun blazed on the deck of the small Boston Whaler sitting idle over its shadow on the white sand bottom twenty feet below. The anchored Whaler was the only boat out on the placid blue surface of the bay, unusual for a Sunday on Isla Colombo. A slowly swimming snorkeler in bright red trunks was returning to the boat from the outer reef. Distracted earlier by a small school of trumpet fish darting around him, Larry Griffin had not seen the jellyfish when he swam over to the reef a half hour ago, and he did not see them now. The pain hit him like a blast from a flamethrower. The air bursting out of his lungs blew the snorkel out of his mouth as he reflexively arched partway up out of the water, startling several sunbathers over on the beach. As Griffin choked and clawed in a frantic dog paddle, a young couple dragged a kayak down off the beach and started paddling toward him. Griffin somehow made it the last few yards to the boat and pulled himself up over the gunwale. Everything went numb as he lost consciousness.

Forty-eight hours later, Griffin was hallucinating as he regained consciousness in the infirmary of the Medical College of Isla Colombo, where he was a second-year medical student. The hallucinations slowly gave way to increasing awareness of the muffled sighs of the breathing support apparatus and the rhythmic beep of the heart monitor. He grappled with his first real thoughts, which began with a vague memory of the jellyfish tentacles clinging to his face, shoulders, arms, and chest just before passing out in the boat. Now he remembered hearing somewhere about a prediction that worldwide overfishing of top predator species including sharks would eventually cause jellyfish to dominate the predator niche in the oceans. He hated the thought that the goddamn environmental scientists might be right. His scorn for environmental scientists stemmed directly from his painful memories of being dismissed from a graduate program in freshwater ecology up in Michigan two years earlier on charges of sexual harassment of two students while he was a teaching assistant in an introductory biology lab section. He had then applied to this second-rate Caribbean med school and had succeeded in getting in, although just barely.

Griffin's thoughts were interrupted when two nurses entered his room and began taking his vital signs. One of them was an attractive young mestiza, native to the island. As Juanita gazed at Griffin's deeply tanned face and wavy dark hair, tears brimmed at the corners of her almond eyes. She had seen him in a bed several times before—her own bed actually, and she had been in it with him, unable to resist the urgent allure of his dark brown eyes and tanned muscular body. His eyes still closed, Griffin recognized Juanita's voice as she spoke to the other nurse, apparently unaware that Griffin was conscious now.

"His reaction to those stings was unusually severe wasn't it?"

"Yeah, nearly fatal, and it's still touch and go," replied the other nurse. "They think it was more of an allergic reaction than purely neurologic damage; the jellyfish in this area are not that toxic."

"Do they think he will recover?"

"Probably. He's lucky he got help quickly."

"Yes."

"And lucky it wasn't the Australian box jelly. That much contact with that species would almost certainly have been fatal within minutes."

The nurses put away the blood pressure equipment and left the room. As Griffin thought about that conversation, the searing pain of the hundreds of stinging welts on his upper body brought into focus the beginnings of an idea.

Two months later, Larry Griffin was enrolled in the gene technology course. From the windows of the second floor lab he could look out on the crystal blue water of the small bay where he had become acquainted with the jellyfish. He applied himself with rapt attention to learning the techniques of identifying, isolating, and transferring a gene from one species to another. The hard parts were identifying and isolating a gene, and happily for Griffin the genes he was interested in had already been obtained by Professor Mendoza, who was teaching this very course.

CHAPTER 1

In the third week of June the tourist season had barely gotten started in Traverse City, Michigan. After a quick breakfast on a cool Friday morning, environmental attorney Craig Basham threw a jacket over his blue button-down shirt, stepped off the front porch of his lavender Victorian "painted lady" and walked at his usual brisk pace along the several blocks to his office. There was not a cloud in the sky, and songbirds were in full voice in the maples lining the street. Craig, a stocky six-two with a blond crewcut, was lost in thought and did not tune in to the splendid setting the way he normally would. Entering his second floor office on Washington Street, he laid his morning paper on his desk and dialed his friend Paul Tyson. Tyson was a postdoctoral researcher at the nearby Rynar University Limnology Institute, known by its acronym as RULI.

Paul set down his morning coffee on the cockpit table of his boat, looked at his caller ID, and took the call. "What's up, you tree hugger puke?"

"Well gee Paul, what does that make you, an algae hugger puke? And how the hell do you hug algae? Anyway, have you seen the article in this morning's paper about the otters at Whitetail Lake?"

"I don't read the paper. What otters?"

"Several have been found dead in the lake over the last couple of weeks."

"Otters have a tendency to do that, not unlike all living things, counselor."

Craig shook his head. "Come on smartass, this is an unusual set of mortalities, and it's not happening in any other lakes and ponds in the area. I'm concerned that there might be some illegal dumping of something toxic going on there." Basham made his living litigating against those who trash the environment, and his radar for potential cases did not have an off switch.

"Well I don't know much about otters," replied Tyson. "I'm just a phytoplankton guy, but I'll check with my animal biologist friends here at RULI. And I guess I could take a look at the water chemistry there. Where is this lake?"

"About ten miles southeast of town, off Garfield Road. There is a public access boat ramp."

"What's it called again?"

"Whitetail Lake."

"Gotcha."

"Okay, thanks Paul." Craig Basham rang off.

Paul Tyson, who had been Craig Basham's roommate in undergrad college at Northwestern, studied planktonic algae in Lake Michigan. He had finished his Ph.D. here at RULI last year and stayed on as a postdoctoral research associate in the lab of his mentor, Dr. Walter Perry. Perry was now an emeritus professor, and he relied on Tyson for day-to-day management of the lab's research programs in limnology, better known as freshwater ecology, that had been continuously funded by federal grants for over three decades. Tyson continued his studies of the effects of global warming on the phytoplankton algae in northern Lake Michigan. Now in his mid-thirties with some premature grey flecks already appearing in his coarse brown hair, he was still in nearly as good shape as he was in his high school football days that produced the scar along the angle of his strong jaw. He lived aboard a sailboat in Elk Rapids harbor on the east side of

Grand Traverse Bay's East Arm, and commuted to the institute at the foot of the West Arm of the bay in Traverse City.

Paul changed from his sleeping shorts to his usual cargo shorts, tee shirt and RULI ball cap, ate a quick breakfast, and finished what was left in his coffee pot while watching the sun-warmed morning dew steam up off of the wood planks of the dock alongside his boat. He locked up the boat, walked over to his red '66 Mustang GT coupe and drove up onto River Street and over to U.S. 31. Southward along the short fifteen miles to Traverse, the endless rows of orchard trees were beginning to get serious about producing the summer crop of cherries, and the East Arm of the bay gleamed in the morning sun.

Arriving at the Rynar University campus at the foot of Old Mission Peninsula, Paul parked at the Limnology Institute on West Bay and saw that the two research vessels were in the harbor at their usual moorings. The 35-foot *Chinook* rocked gently to the slight harbor swell, while the 115-foot *Halcyon* was virtually motionless while a couple of deckhands worked on a large winch on the foredeck. Paul waved to the two young men and entered the limnology building that served as the institute headquarters. He dropped off his laptop case at his desk in Dr. Perry's lab, noticed that Dr. Perry was not in his office yet, and walked over next door to the biology building, where Joan Brockton was in her mentor's lab working on her doctoral dissertation research. Paul knocked on the open lab door and entered.

"Hey, Joanie."

Joan rose from her chair with a grin, shook back her honey-brown hair, and exchanged a quick kiss with Paul.

"What brings you over here so early in the morning, Paul?"

"Got a question. Among your animal biology brethren here, who would know best about otters?"

"That would be Dr. Casey upstairs. He's a mammalogist specializing in aquatic species. Why would you want to know that?"

"Craig Basham called me this morning about some otters that have been dying in nearby Whitetail Lake. Wonders if there is a pollution problem involved. If there is, he'll be on it like a pit bull on a meat wagon."

"Well, let's go upstairs and see if Dr. Casey knows anything about it."

As they left Joan's lab, she made sure the door was locked; even here in the idyllic north country there was always risk of a quick strike by someone interested in lab reagents that can be used to make street drugs, or lab equipment useful in processing and weighing out drugs, not to mention purses and laptops. They climbed the stairs to the 2nd floor and entered the lab of Dr. Robert Casey, who lo-and-behold was at that very moment performing a necropsy on an otter.

"Excuse us, Dr. Casey," said Joan.

"Oh, hello Joan. And Paul, is it?"

"That's me," replied Paul. "I just learned about some otter fatalities in Whitetail Lake, and wondered if you know anything about them."

"Well, as a matter of fact, this is one of them right here. A guy from the Whitetail Lake homeowners association called me yesterday and brought two of them here to see if I can discover anything unusual about their deaths."

"What are you seeing?" asked Joan.

"There's no external trauma from a dog or other predator attack, but there is some inflammation of the mouth and nasal areas. Internally there are some more obvious problems. There is cerebral and pulmonary edema, which I assume you know is swelling from fluid engorgement that may indicate acute hypertension. The blood analysis yesterday showed pretty severe cytopenia, the loss of blood cells. However, the blood chemistry showed no presence of toxins that we normally test for, including heavy metals and organic poisons. So we don't know what caused this; maybe some kind of infection, but microbial analyses will take a little more time, and if it's a virus we may never know."

"Okay," said Paul. "I guess Craig Basham will have to cool his heels on the pollution angle, at least for now."

"That's that environmental lawyer, right?" replied Dr. Casey. "I hear he is very good. Glad to have him on deck if and when we need some legal muscle."

Paul smiled. "Muscle is a good description. He was a hell of a linebacker at Northwestern in his day. Fire-in-the-belly's still there. Anyway, could you give me a list of the toxins that your lab tests for?"

"Yes, here's one right here; I'll print out another copy for myself later."

"Thanks Dr. Casey. I guess we'll check back in a few days to see if the microbiology shows anything."

"Monday or Tuesday should do it," replied Casey.

Paul walked Joan back down to her lab. Just as he was leaving to return to his own lab, a thought came to him.

"You know what, I've finally finished de-winterizing *Tondeleyo* for the summer season." He was talking about the 41-foot center-cockpit ketch that was his home. "What say we go for a sail tomorrow, maybe overnight somewhere?"

Joan thought a minute as she surveyed the stacks of data notebooks and graphs on her desk. "Yes, that would be a nice break from this stuff. It's going well, but coming up for air now and then is a good idea."

"That's true, and it's supposed to be nice for the next couple of days. Come on up in the morning for breakfast, and we'll decide where to go."

"Deal," replied Joan.

"Good. Right now I'm going to drive out to Whitetail Lake and get a water sample. I want to run it through our water analysis facility to see if there is something there that Dr. Casey's blood work doesn't test for."

"Okay, Paul, see you later."

Chapter 2

Returning to the limnology building, Paul found that Dr. Perry was in his office now. As a semi-retired emeritus professor, Perry was no longer teaching and did not keep regular hours. He did continue to publish the on-going research which now was supported by federal grants written jointly with Paul. Paul stopped in to tell Perry about the otter deaths and his plan to get some samples at Whitetail Lake.

"Why don't you take Brad with you," said Perry. "The more exposure he can get to what we do, the better." All new grad students served rotations in three faculty labs during their first year, and Bradley Barlow was doing his third one here in Dr. Perry's lab. Barlow, a short slender fellow with spiked yellow hair and a couple of earrings in one ear, was at the lab sink washing glassware. Paul approached him.

"Hi Brad. Want to go with me out to Whitetail Lake for a water sample? There have been some mysterious otter fatalities there, and we need to help look into the situation."

"Anything to get away from this sink," replied Brad.

Paul wondered for a moment about the kid's level of commitment, but what the hell, who likes cleanup duty. Paul collected some plastic sample bottles, and decided to bring a small Wisconsin plankton net and an Ekman bottom sediment sampler as well. He wanted to see if there were any unusual algal blooms going on in the lake. He and Brad went out to Paul's car, loaded the equipment in the trunk, and drove over to nearby Garfield Road. They headed south past the airport and out of town, where the road jogged southeastward for a number of miles and gradually entered a wooded area of typical northern hardwoods and evergreens interspersed with wildflower meadows. Paul turned at the sign for Whitetail Lake and followed the gravel road for a half-mile to the public access boat ramp. They parked in the small lot and carried the equipment out onto the dock alongside the ramp that extended several yards out into the lake.

Paul took a moment to look out around the lake, which was forested right to its edge with an attractive mix of cedar, hemlock and pine, and there were a number of modest homes scattered around it.

"Pretty little lake," said Paul. "A typical kettle lake left over from melted glacial ice blocks, like many of the small lakes in Michigan. Looks to be about six or eight hectares in surface area."

"How big is a hectare again?" asked Barlow.

"Ten thousand square meters, a little more than twice an acre. So the lake is around twelve acres. You might want to call it a big pond, but these things are pretty deep and become thermally stratified in summer like larger lakes do."

"Meaning that there is a layer of sun-warmed water on top of cold water below the thermocline, right?"

"You're getting your limnology down well, my friend."

"I'm working on it," said Barlow. "By the way, what is the term limnolgy derived from?"

"From the Greek, *limnos*, for lake or inland waterway."

"The water here looks pretty clear, doesn't it?" said Barlow.

"Yes it does. One thing here is unusual for small lakes like this with lakefront homes around them: these homeowners have the sense to allow natural vegetation to persist along their waterfronts, rather than insisting on manicured grass lawns right to the water's edge. No fertilizing, and therefore no hyper-eutrophication and no massive algal mess. It's very simple and effective for sustaining healthy lakes. Anyway, let's get going. While I get this plankton sample, you can fill those two one-liter water sample bottles here near the end of the dock. If anyone is dumping something, it would probably be right here. Quick in and out for their vehicle."

Paul uncoiled the line attached to the plankton net and looped the end around his wrist. He swung the net around his head like a lariat and threw it as far as he could out into the lake, pulling it back to him just fast enough to keep it from sinking to the bottom. He threw it twice more, and then emptied the plankton-filled water that remained in the cup at the end of the net into a small plastic bottle. He coiled the line, rinsed the net in the lake, and packed it in its carrying case. These nets were not used for research much anymore, partly because they were not sufficiently quantitative and mostly because they missed the really small "nannoplankton" and "picoplankton" that were very important components of the algal community. But they were useful for introductory teaching and for quick qualitative sampling of the common larger species.

The two of them then operated the Ekman sampler to grab some bottom sediment, which they rinsed into a bucket. Paul wanted to have that analyzed for pollutants as well.

"Okay, let's pack up and get back," said Paul.

"Yep," replied Barlow. "Hey Paul, what are those things over there that look like unused condoms?" Three flimsy, milky-white circular objects a little larger than a quarter coin were slowly drifting just below the surface of the water not far from the dock. "Why would anyone throw away unused condoms?" wondered Barlow. Paul agreed that they vaguely resembled the rolled-up prophylactics that came in foil packs. But that's not what these were.

"Well I'll be damned," said Paul. "Those are freshwater jellyfish. The only time I've ever seen those was in a small pond over in Illinois while I was an undergrad. They're not usually very abundant in this region, but can appear in some numbers now and then especially in smaller ponds. They don't get any bigger than that, and they're dangerous only to the zooplankton that they feed on. Well, let's get back to the lab."

Back at the institute, Paul took the two water sample bottles and the bucket of sediment into the core facility for water analysis and asked the technician to run a full chemical analysis including a complete toxin profile, explaining the situation out at Whitetail Lake and the need for as quick a turn-around as possible. The tech agreed and got to work.

Paul returned to his lab and put a couple of drops of the phytoplankton sample on a glass slide and looked at it under a microscope. He was looking for unusually large numbers of either blue-green algae or dinoflagellates, both of which could include species that are quite toxic. He did not see any evidence of that, only a standard mix of green algae, diatoms, and others including only a few blue-greens and dinoflagellates. Paul let Brad Barlow take a look.

"That's a normal algal community for a healthy small lake in this region," said Paul. "Toxic algae are clearly not the problem in Whitetail Lake."

Paul washed the slide and put the sample bottle in the refrigerator, and Brad went back to finish his work at the sink. Paul went to his desk, pulled out a sandwich from his laptop case, and turned his attention to his Lake Michigan research data.

At five p.m. Paul closed up the lab and drove back up to Elk Rapids under a still-sunny sky; these were the longest days of the year and the sun was still high in the late afternoon. He stopped on River Street and picked up a hot Italian sandwich and a slice of pizza and brought them down to his boat where there was cold beer in the fridge. He enjoyed his meal in the cockpit and had a second beer while watching the pinks and purples of evening settle over the quiet harbor. After an hour or two of reading one of his paperback "boat books" down in the salon, he hit the rack for the night.

Chapter 3

Joan Brockton looked out of the bay window of her second-story apartment on Front Street and saw that Saturday morning had dawned clear and breezy with small whitecaps out on West Bay. A perfect day for a sail. It would be chilly out there, so she added a sweater to her small backpack containing a few overnight items, grabbed a jacket, and went down to her white Chevy Blazer in the parking lot. The fifteen mile drive up U.S. 31 to Elk Rapids was pleasant with little traffic.

Joan was a 30-year-old third-year doctoral student studying Coho salmon ecophysiology and genetics. She had isolated the genes that control the fish's osmotic control in the transition from freshwater to salt water in the Pacific coast life cycle, and was doing experiments to determine how those genes functioned in absence of a saltwater phase in the Great Lakes. She had gotten to know Paul Tyson during her first year and they had become very close, especially that summer when the disastrous fatality on the *Halcyon* had nearly landed Paul in prison for life.

She stopped at a coffee shop on River Street in Elk Rapids and picked up a bag-full of warm fresh bagels with cream cheese and strawberry jam. She drove down into the marina lot below the bright white Island House library and parked beside Paul's Mustang. She saw Paul hosing down the deck of his boat in its slip at the seawall, and she tapped the horn a couple of times as she got out with her backpack and locked the truck. Paul shut off the deck hose and watched her walk across the grass to the seawall. She was stunning as ever in her teal Bahama sailing shirt and faded jeans, her golden pony tail trailing out of the gap in the back of her royal blue RULI ball cap. Paul loved ball caps on women, especially on Joan.

"Permission to come aboard, Captain?"

"By all means. That bag from the coffee shop looks interesting."

Joan stepped on deck between the stanchions at the open boarding gap in the lifelines and handed Paul the bag of bagels. He opened the bag and savored the aroma while she dropped her jacket onto the portside cockpit bench and took her backpack below. Paul followed her down and grabbed her in a hug from behind. She twisted around to face him and returned the hug.

"Haven't seen enough of you lately, young lady," said Paul.

"Teaching this early summer session has me way too tied up." Joan was a teaching assistant in the introductory biology course.

"Like my dad says, it's hell to be poor and have to *work* for a living," replied Paul.

"As though you hotshot postdocs actually work for your big bucks!" retorted Joan.

"Yeah right. We just sit around watching you grad students do all the work."

Paul got a couple of hardboiled eggs out of the fridge to go with the bagels, poured a couple of mugs from the coffee-maker carafe, and they went back up to the cockpit to eat. The sun was high enough to generate some real warmth, but it had competition from the fresh west wind coming across the cold water of East Bay. White gulls wheeled and bleated back and forth over the marina, chasing one of their flock that had a big hunk of bread in its beak with no apparent intention of sharing it. The muffled roar of the Elk River water piling through the small power dam into the harbor was barely audible in the wind.

"Still a lot of empty slips," said Joan as she watched several boaters lugging pushcarts full of gear out along the docks to outfit their boats for the season.

"It's early in the season; they'll all fill up," Paul replied. "This marina is perpetually fully subscribed with a waiting list as long as your arm. Elk Rapids is getting known as of one of the nicest harbor towns on Lake Michigan. But in my opinion we're lucky that being this far down on the east side of the bay it is a little too far off the direct path from the more northerly ports of Harbor Springs and Charlevoix and the others south along Lake Michigan's east shore; keeps us from being so overrun like those others can be. Nice quiet intimate place."

Joan nodded, and they munched bagels and sipped coffee in silence for a bit. Then she asked, "Do you think there's anything to that dead otter business?"

"Probably nothing more than some kind of epizootic disease. But those things can get serious, like for instance the fungal infections that seem to be at least part of the decline of amphibians everywhere in the world."

"Oh my. Let's hope not. Anyway, where are you taking me today, you piratical scallywag?"

"How about sailing over to Sutton's Bay for an overnight. There's an early-season art fair on the waterfront there this weekend, and some good restaurants."

"Sounds perfect."

They went below, cleaned and stored the coffee maker and mugs, and secured everything for seagoing motion. Back on deck Paul started the engine to let it warm up. Joan unzipped the StackPack sail covers while Paul unhooked the shore power cables and water hose from the service stanchion at the head of the slip. The boat did not need fuel, as it had been filled at the end of last season and this was the first time out since then. But the holding tank for the head was full, so after slipping the dock lines and backing out of the slip, Paul stopped at the fuel dock for pumpout service. Several people on the docks stopped what they were doing and watched as Paul's magnificent forty-one-foot center cockpit ketch slowly motored through the channel between the breakwaters. *Tondeleyo* was a favorite in the harbor, with her gleaming black hull, gold stripe and scrollwork along the hull below the railing, and white decks and cabin tops. Paul had the astonishing good fortune to have inherited the boat from his old friend and sailing mentor, the famous but childless author Ian Kerrigan.

Clearing the breakwaters, Paul turned left into the wind and continued motoring slowly, giving the wheel to Joan. He raised the mizzen sail at the stern first as a weather vane to help Joan keep the boat headed into the wind, and then the big mainsail. Both sails rattled and shook as he cranked out the roller jib, which added its own rattle and roar. Joan turned the boat back northward and the sails went silent as they filled and drew strongly on a port tack. Paul took the wheel and shut off the engine. Joan braced herself against the moderate heel to starboard and grinned as she gazed past the canted white sails to the bright blue landless horizon of northern Lake Michigan stretching beyond the head of Traverse Bay.

"There is nothing," quoted Joan from *The Wind in the Willows*, "absolutely nothing quite so much worth doing as simply messing about in boats."

"And this," replied Paul, "is the best of it."

They sailed in a broad reach at five knots in the ten knot breeze for a couple of hours until noon when they came abreast of the tip of Old Mission Peninsula on their left. While they worked another mile to the north of the shoals there, they ate peanut butter sandwiches and some fruit. They turned left toward the west and began the tacking they would have to do to get across the head of West Arm to where Suttons Bay lay, directly upwind of them. Three tacks and two hours later they entered Suttons Bay, which was calm because it was in the lee of the Leelanau Peninsula. They lowered sails and motored to an anchorage near the breakwater of the town's harbor. There was no need to bother with getting a slip in the marina; the wind would be from the west all weekend and the anchorage would be well protected here.

After setting the anchor and shutting down the engine, they closed and locked the hatchway door and lowered the dingy from its stern davits. They rowed over to a small beach next to the breakwater, pulled the dingy up on the sand, and walked over to the art fair. The white canvass tents were lined up in two rows, some with displays and racks of paintings or photos and most with various craft knickknacks and carvings. They wandered along among the small crowd and stopped at many of the tents, and Joan bought a wooden toy for her niece who lived in Farmington Hills near Detroit. At the last tent they realized that they were hungry enough for dinner already, even though it was only five-thirty. They walked up to the main drag and found a likely looking pub and went inside for burgers and beer. It was good to get in out of the cool wind, and the first glass of draft Blue Light went down quickly.

CHAPTER 4

While Paul and Joan were having dinner in Suttons Bay, a twelve-year old boy was playing with his dog along the shore down on Whitetail Lake. Kevin Sarginson dearly loved Buck, a three-year-old yellow lab who never tired of retrieving sticks thrown out in the water. Kevin had been throwing a stick for Buck for only a few minutes when the dog yelped on his way out for the latest toss. He turned back toward shore yelping and choking on water.

"What's wrong Buck?" shouted Kevin. "Buck?"

The dog slowed down and barely made it to shore. He crawled partway out on the sand and collapsed. Kevin ran to him. Buck was struggling for breath.

"Dad, Mom," cried Kevin at he ran up to the house. Kevin's Dad came out.

"Something's wrong with Buck," said Kevin.

His dad followed him down to the beach, where he found that Buck was no longer breathing and appeared to be dead. The dad rushed back to the house, found the emergency number for their vet, and got the OK to meet the vet at his clinic. Kevin sobbed as his dad carried Buck to the Chevy Tahoe and laid him in the back compartment, and they drove to the vet. The vet tried in vain to resuscitate the dog.

"I'm sorry," said the vet. "What happened?"

"He just started yelping when he was swimming, and fell down when he got to the beach," replied Kevin.

"I can't find anything wrong externally, except some inflammation in his mouth and nose. Had he been sick or eaten something other than his normal food?"

"No, I don't think so," replied Kevin's dad. "Kevin, have you seen Buck eating mushrooms in the woods or anything like that?"

"No," said Kevin.

"We don't led Buck roam free," Kevin's dad said to the vet, "so I don't think he has gotten into any poisons that someone may have put out for rodents or anything like that."

"He could have had a heart attack, but he's too young for that," said the vet. "If you want, I can do a necropsy, but it's a bit expensive."

The dad answered, "You know, the association has sent some otters that were found dead here to the university to be checked out; maybe they would look at Buck too."

"Good idea. I'll put him in our cold box until Monday for you."

"Thanks very much, doc."

Kevin sobbed again as his dad led him back out to the truck. On the way home the dad called the neighbor who was dealing with the otters. The neighbor was sorry to hear about Buck, said he was a fine dog, and he would call Dr. Casey at the university.

Kevin was too upset to eat much at dinner, and he went down to the shore to where Buck had died and sat on a stump. He stared at the lake for hours, wishing that the vet had been mistaken and that he would bring Buck back to the house alive. But Buck did not come bounding down to the lake. Kevin threw one of Buck's favorite sticks out on the water and watched it float around motionless. He watched for a while and then picked up a rock and hurled it at the stick. He missed, and the stick just sat there, reminding Kevin more than ever of his loss.

Eventually the stick faded from view as darkness fell. Kevin stood up to go back to the house, but as he turned he noticed something in the lake that he had never seen before. Small circles of pale green light were drifting around under the surface, as though fireflies had been squashed with their lights still on and dumped in the lake. But these things were moving, undulating slightly as they rose and fell in the water column. It was so intriguing that Kevin momentarily forgot about Buck. He wished he could run over to tell his friend Ryan about it, but Ryan and his family would not be arriving at their nearby cottage for another week. Kevin decided not to tell anyone else about what he was seeing. He wanted to wait for Ryan so they could catch some of the weird things and surprise everyone.

    Kevin's thoughts returned to Buck as he trudged up to the house.

Chapter 5

Paul and Joan finished their burgers in the Suttons Bay pub and walked back down to the waterfront, shoved the dingy back in the water and rowed out to *Tondeleyo*. At seven p.m. the sun was still high in the sky; in June at this latitude and this far west in the eastern time zone it doesn't get dark until nearly 10 pm. They opened a couple of bottles of Blue Moon and sat in the cockpit and watched the various boaters and jet skiers taking advantage of the pleasant evening. Later down in the salon they played some rummy for a half hour, and then went back up to the cockpit to watch the lights winking on in town and the moon rising from behind Old Mission Peninsula.

They stood and embraced, and Joan said, "Hmm… I notice as usual that you have no need for the little blue pills."

"Not unless you're interested in a four hour marathon."

"Interesting idea. But no. Somewhere between that and four minutes would be good."

They went below.

In the morning they rowed back ashore and found a restaurant that advertised the "best breakfast on the bay" and were leisurely enjoying mountains of blueberry pancakes when Paul's cell phone rang. The caller ID said Craig Basham was calling again. Paul hit the talk key.

"Dude, can't a guy get a little peace on a Sunday morning?"

"Sorry Paul," replied Craig. "But a story on local TV news this morning got my attention and is making me nervous as hell. A kid's yellow lab died suddenly while swimming in Whitetail Lake yesterday afternoon, with no apparent cause other than inflammation of its mouth and nose areas. The dog is going to be examined further tomorrow at the university, apparently by the same guy that is looking at the otters. What the hell is going on?"

"Hmm," mused Paul, furrowing his brow and pursing his lips. "Had the dog's mouth been inflamed for a while?"

"They didn't say, but I got the impression that the whole thing was out of the blue and unexpected."

"Well I will be talking to Dr. Casey tomorrow about the otter situation, so I'll be getting up to date on the dog too. Doesn't sound like a chronic poisoning thing, does it?"

"I guess not. Let me know what you learn. Thanks Paul, sorry to interrupt your morning in beautiful Elk Rapids."

"Actually you interrupted a great breakfast with Joan over here in Suttons Bay, but we'll recover. Talk to you later."

Paul hit the end-call key and answered Joan's questioning look. "We're getting otters and dogs now in Whitetail Lake. Some poor kid's yellow lab."

"Oh that's sad," said Joan. "My favorite breed."

"Mine too. Super dogs."

They finished their hotcakes, washed them down with one more cup of coffee, and left the restaurant agreeing that it might well be the "best breakfast on the bay" as advertised. They strolled down past the art fair area, which was not yet open for business. They went straight to the dingy at the beach and rowed back out to *Tondeleyo* sitting idly at her anchor line on the flat water. They weighed anchor and motored out of the bay until they got into the west wind that was coming over the Leelanau Peninsula. With all sails up and drawing they turned northward on a broad reach and aimed toward Charlevoix. Halfway there they jibed around and headed back southward on a starboard broad reach toward Elk Rapids. It was tempting to go on to Charlevoix for another overnight, but they had too much to do tomorrow.

They ate peanut butter sandwiches and fruit again for lunch as *Tondeleyo* glided along past the sun-washed woods lining both shores of the bay. The young pale-green leaves of the birches, maples and beeches contrasted with the darker green of the pines, hemlocks and cedars. That early evening, with *Tondeleyo* all tied up in her home slip and sail covers zipped up, Paul and Joan sat in the fading sunshine eating Italian sandwiches and pizza from River Street. Joan took a swig of Corona, and looked at her watch. Noticing the date, she blinked, raised her eyebrows and looked at Paul.

"Do you realize that it is already two years almost to the day since the Ron Withers tragedy started on the *Halcyon*?"

"Well, it started before that when he plagiarized my data and I publically threatened him about it, but yeah, that's when the shit really hit the fan."

They were talking about the events that the media had called the "Halcyon Fury Affair." Paul had nearly been convicted of murder after fellow student Ronald Withers had been fatally injured on a research cruise.

"I hope poor Ron's family is doing okay now after losing him like that," said Joan. "Same for the families of the two guys that died trying to ram us with their truck, just because they lost a fight they picked with you in jail."

"Thanks for the reminder. I heard that one of them had a younger brother that's around town somewhere."

"He's never been a problem has he?"

"Not yet, at least. And as long as we're basking in pleasant memories, how about your friend Larry Griffin? What do you suppose he is up to these days?"

Joan grimaced and shook her head violently. "Oh Paul, that was the worst night of my life. He came very close to raping me. And later the bastard came close to getting you convicted with his bogus testimony."

"Later your testimony helped get him get kicked out of RULI for molesting those girls in his lab. Where did he end up after that?"

"I heard something about med school somewhere, but I don't know where or how he got in. Can you imagine him as a doctor? Good god."

Chapter 6

At the time that Paul and Joan were chatting on *Tondeleyo*, dusk was settling over the beach down on Isla Colombo where Larry Griffin was sitting in blue-patterned surfer trunks and a tank top on the balcony of his second-floor student apartment sucking on a bottle of local rum. Tanned and muscular, he used the fitness room on campus regularly, not for health reasons so much as for maximizing his ability to seduce young women, his favorite activity.

Summer heat was already well established on this small independent island nation, which was relatively flat without the high hills of most of the nearby Virgin Islands. It sat to the south of the British Virgin Islands, and was about thirty-five miles southeast of St. Thomas. Its pear shape was only eight miles long from north to south and three to four miles wide from east to west. The med school was in an isolated area on the east coast of the island facing the Atlantic, due east of the only town, Cristobal, which was over on the Caribbean side. In contrast to the better known U.S. and British Virgin Islands, Isla Colombo was unofficially known as the "Spanish Virgin." There was no history of significant agriculture here, and aside from the medical school the only basis for the economy was tourism—especially snorkeling, diving and sport fishing—and several "offshore" banks with strict policies of secrecy about their customers' accounts.

Half a bottle into it, the rum and the warm fragrant air had Griffin thinking about Juanita Salazar, the pretty little five-foot-two nurse that had treated him in the infirmary the previous year when he had almost died of anaphylactic shock from the jellyfish contact. He had been with her several times both before and since then, and he realized now that she was one of his favorite pieces of ass on this "crummy little island," as he would put it. But she had tried to get him to be serious about their relationship, which he had no intention of doing, and he had sought other bed-mates lately. He couldn't get her out of his mind now, and as he hadn't had a romp with any babe in days, he rose from his lounge chair and carried his rum bottle down out of the apartment to his car in the parking lot. He tried to keep the car between the center line and the shoulder on his way over to Juanita's apartment in town.

Juanita answered the knock on her door and drew a sudden breath at the sight of Griffin standing with one hand propped on the door jamb and the other loosely holding the rum bottle. It was as though the model for Michelangelo's David had gotten drunk and showed up at her place. She stared at his deep-set languid eyes, and then looked down along the familiar tan biceps, the ripped abs and narrow hips, the long muscular thighs, and back up to the groin area where a brewing Richter–scale event was producing early warning signals at the National Earthquake Information Center in Colorado.

She stepped back and held the door open for him, letting her breath back out in a small mewing sigh. She seemed to be welcoming him with a smile, but the look in her eyes did not match the smile. Griffin saw the smile. He also saw the shiny black hair cascading down just below her shoulders, the firm swell of her breasts beneath her black sports bra, and the unbelievable curves of her hips under her black Spandex running tights. He couldn't see her backside, his favorite part, so he slid his hand around back there to refresh his memory of it; the feel of it against the thin silky Spandex brought a low groan up out of his throat. *Sweet*

Jesus what a lovely ass. Griffin was now on the verge of rivaling the Mount Saint Helen eruption.

"Where have you been lately?" she said, reaching around and bringing his hand back in front of her, where she held it to her chest.

"Oh, you know, busy as hell at school, exams coming up." Griffin wiped sweat off of his forehead and took a pull on the bottle.

"Do you want something to eat?" Juanita asked.

"I want you. We can eat later."

Juanita bowed her head. "Can't we at least talk first? You know I love to be with you, but I need to know what is in your heart."

"We can talk later too."

Juanita turned toward her bedroom door. Griffin pulled her hand back toward him.

"Just bend over the back of the couch right here, sweetheart."

"Oh Larry, you know I don't like it that way. Come to the bed with me."

"Can't wait babe."

"Please no. And please don't talk to me that way, Larry."

Griffin pulled her over to her small desk and bent her face down over it. The rum bottle slid out of his hand onto the floor as he roughly rearranged their clothing enough to do what he came to do.

"Larry, please, I've tried to enjoy it this way, but it doesn't work."

"Shut up, will you."

The table began pounding against the wall so fast and hard that Juanita's glass-framed nursing degree fell down and smashed on the floor near the rum bottle. The pounding went on.

"Larry, stop, get out of here, you bastard. CABRÓN. CULO. I HATE YOU."

Griffin finished and backed away. "Well to hell with you, you little mestiza bitch."

Griffin walked out of the apartment, and Juanita slumped down to the floor next to Griffin's empty bottle with her hands to her face. She trembled like a palmetto in a hurricane and stared at her broken diploma frame.

As Griffin walked to his car, the echo of Juanita's shouted pleas merged in his mind with a memory of similar cries from his mother behind his parents' bedroom door one afternoon a decade ago, after which his drunken father had come out of the room and said, "What're you lookin' at, shithead," slamming Griffin against the hallway wall with a backhand slap to his face. Griffin quickly shoved that memory back into the dark recesses that were filled with the pain of his past youth in that house, and brought his mind back to the thrill of taking Juanita as he had just done. *I should have done that to that self-righteous Joan Brockton when I had the chance up in Traverse*, thought Griffin as he drove back toward his apartment. He was thinking about the night of his unsuccessful attempt at seducing her in her apartment two years ago. He thought again about the sexual harassment charges that had gotten him kicked out of Rynar University a few weeks later. *All I did was grab their asses a couple of times. What's the big deal?* He gave no further thought to any of those women including Juanita as he stopped for a couple of burritos on the way home.

CHAPTER 7

Back in his apartment, Griffin ate his burritos with a beer, and settled back in his balcony chair to watch the rest of the evening wear on; stars were high in the sky and the warm trade winds blew straight at him out of the east. A sea turtle broached for a breath in the bay and slowly submerged again. The rhythmic wash of the Atlantic waves on the beach got him calmed down and he lapsed into a pleasing reverie of his successful activities over the past year. Activities that had absorbed so much of his time and energy that he was barely passing his med school courses.

After recovering rapidly from the allergic trauma caused by his contact with the jellyfish off the med school's waterfront a year ago, he had set in motion the plan that had come to him in the infirmary bed. He knew that while the stinging barbs of the tentacles of the jellyfish that he had encountered produced very painful stings, they and most other marine jellyfish were usually not mortally dangerous, at least to fully grown humans. He also knew, however, that the box jelly, or sea wasp, of the Western Pacific carried lethally powerful toxins that could kill an adult human in minutes.

Griffin was also very familiar with so-called freshwater jellyfish, as he had worked with them while he was a teaching assistant in introductory biology at the university in Traverse City, where live cultures of them were provided in the lab classes as demonstrations representing the cnidarian phylum. This species, *Craspedacusta sowerbyi*, is not a true jellyfish because of an anatomical detail, but it is very closely related to jellyfish. In contrast to the much larger true marine jellyfish, the freshwater "jelly" is only between two and three centimeters in diameter as an adult, with short tentacles that they use to kill and feed themselves with zooplankton such as rotifers, copepods, and cladoceran "water fleas."

While the freshwater jelly can be inadvertently harmful or fatal to small fish (such as guppies and other aquarium fish), Griffin knew that they are virtually harmless to large animals including humans because they are so small and have relatively weak stinging barbs and toxins, either failing to penetrate the skin or causing mild irritation at most. But if he could transfer one or more of the box jelly toxin genes into a culture of freshwater jellyfish, maybe he could wreak all sorts of havoc in Traverse City and settle Joan Brockton's hash once and for all. In his mind, Joan, the institute, and the university had humiliated him beyond tolerance; he was far too self-centered to have any inkling that it was actually the other way around.

Griffin knew enough about gene technology to know that making transgenic species was nearly a routine process now. He did not have the training to do this, but there was an opportunity to get the training right there at his med school. Griffin's recovery from the infirmary had coincided nicely with the beginning of a new term, and he jumped at the chance to enroll in the gene technology course, which of course was oriented toward gene therapy techniques in medicine.

Griffin knew from his undergrad biology courses that for all gene technologies, the fundamental tools discovered and developed in the last few decades of the 1900s included two types of enzymes: restriction enzymes isolated from some bacteria that had evolved them to carve up DNA of viruses that attack them, and ligase enzymes that all cells use to attach fragments of DNA during DNA replication for cell reproduction. These enzymes, which one can now buy off the shelf from any of several biotech companies, work the same way on the DNA from any and all species from bacteria to humans and can be used to cut and paste genes from any species into any other species, because DNA in all species is the same in terms of its chemical genetic code. Griffin was also familiar in general with how one can find the location of a specific gene in a species' DNA, extract that gene, produce quantities of it, and introduce it into the DNA of another species, and he applied himself intensely in learning and mastering the details.

Griffin learned the basic techniques of mapping the genome of a species by cutting it into fragments, analyzing the sequence of the four "letters" of the genetic code in each fragment, and determining with a computer how the fragments are lined up in the intact DNA. He learned how to compare the genomes of two related species and find the unique segment that corresponds with a trait that only one of them has. Usually there were several sequences that could be the gene in question, and these putative genes had to be tested for their function by several techniques including making "knockout" versions of individuals that lacked one of the putative sequences to see if it now lacked the trait in question. These were laborious, time-consuming processes that Griffin thankfully did not actually have to perform to get the genes he wanted.

The professor teaching the course, Dr. Manuel Mendoza, was doing research on the use of toxins of the box jelly to develop pharmaceutically useful medical treatments ranging from pain control to heart disease and cancer. Medoza had been trained at the renowned Centre for Genetic Engineering and Biotechnology in Cuba. A friend and classmate from the Centre, who was now in Australia, had obtained four genes for proteins in *Chironex fleckeri* that caused destruction of cells of the blood, nerves and heart, basically through abnormalities in sodium and calcium ion transport. The genes had been isolated and inserted into plasmids, the small circles of bacterial DNA that were the common vehicle for gene transfer. The plasmids could be simply mailed to Mendoza and then used to transfer the genes into any organism to express the genes as the proteins. Dr. Mendoza put the genes into bacteria to generate useful quantities of the proteins for doing research. Griffin wanted to put them into freshwater jellies for creating mayhem.

Griffin got permission to make transgenic freshwater jellyfish with the box jelly toxins for his class term project by telling Dr. Mendoza that culturing freshwater jellies was easy and that therefore they would be useful in studying the ecophysiology of box jelly predation in the laboratory. Griffin did not actually know if freshwater jellies were easy to culture (and later came to learn otherwise), but Mendoza bought the idea and actually encouraged Griffin, giving him bench space in Mendoza's research lab.

The next step was learning how to transfect the genes. In the course, Griffin learned the two techniques common for many years now: the transfer of transgenic plasmids by bacterial infection of a target species, especially for transgenic plants, and the transfer of a gene via a virus given the gene and induced to infect the target organism, the latter having been used in the first successful cure of a human genetic disease. But these techniques often have major limitations, and it would be difficult to find and isolate a bacterium or virus that would infect the freshwater jellies.

However, Dr. Mendoza also taught the more recent technique of direct microinjection of plasmids into cells, tissues and even small whole animals, with the aid of electroporation which enhances membrane permeability by exposure with a strong electrical field. Young freshwater jellies were small enough to be subjected to this process, as had been shown in flatworms earlier. Plasmids engineered to contain transposon vector genes could then penetrate into the nucleus of any cells and transfer the toxin genes into the animal's DNA. Any sperm and egg cells which received the plasmids could then produce generations of transgenic offspring. Griffin jumped all over this technique and got good at it.

All of this went well for Griffin until he started working with the freshwater jellyfish. He placed an order for a culture of the animals from Baines Biological Supply in Mississippi, which supplied the ones used in the intro labs he had taught at Rynar University in Michigan. He searched on line for culturing techniques for this species, and the web sites all indicated that it is difficult to do. He tried it and found that to be an understatement. But he persevered and got good at this too. He maintained a series of generations of them in large cylindrical glass water tanks with gentle aeration and stirring, and fed them with cultures of cladoceran zooplankton which he also bought from Baines Biological.

The adult transgenic animals, which are in the life cycle phase known as the medusa, produced and fertilized their transgenic eggs, which developed into small oval larvae known as planulae; the planulae attached to the bottom of the tank and developed into stationary polyps, which reproduced by budding off into tiny new medusae. To be sure that he had transgenic animals, Griffin had included a commonly-used marker gene in the plasmids which was the gene for bioluminescence, isolated years ago from another species of marine jellyfish. All he had to do to check which individuals were successfully transgenic was to turn the lights off at night. Those that had the new genes glowed with a pale green light. He could pick those out and separate them from the non-glowing individuals.

Finally he had fully transgenic cultures. It was time to set in motion the rest of his plan.

CHAPTER 8

Six weeks before the otters started dying in Whitetail Lake, Jerry Fenner had been driving his white Ford F150 pickup past the Rynar University Limnology Institute along Bay Shore Drive every weekday at quitting time since the construction company he worked for began renovating a house west of town. Every time he passed the institute he looked out at the dock where his older brother Jake had been killed two years ago when his truck crashed against a mooring bollard and flipped into the bay. Jerry had never fully understood what had happened, but he knew that Paul Tyson and Joan Brockton were involved somehow, mostly Tyson. Jerry, who now resembled his brother with his beer paunch, long dark hair and grimy tee shirt, had recently bought a truck like his brother's, one that was a little newer and not so beat up. Jake was gone, and the best Jerry could do was try to be like him. One day as he was passing the institute his cell phone rang.
"Yeah?"
"Is this Jerry Fenner?"
"Who's asking?"
"I'm Larry Griffin. I was a friend of your brother." That was a bit of a stretch, but Griffin had talked to Jake once and given him information about Paul Tyson. "I'm looking to get even with Joan Brockton and her pal Paul Tyson, along with that tinhorn college there. Tyson's the guy who busted up

your brother and his friend in jail two years ago. Brockton got me kicked out of the institute."

"I'm interested. But how do you know who I am, and how did you get my number?"

"Anybody with a computer and an Internet connection can find out anything, dude."

"Where are you calling from?"

"Isla Colombo in the Caribbean."

Well la de da, thought Fenner. "Okay. I'm listening."

"Through the miracle of science I have created a transgenic freshwater jellyfish that…"

"Whoa, whoa. You lost me already. You're not speaking English. Start over."

"Okay. I'm at a medical school on this god-forsaken island. I have changed a harmless freshwater jellyfish into one that packs a wallop like marine jellyfish do. With me now?"

"Yeah."

"I want to plant these things in a small lake near Traverse City and see if they will grow there and cause some trouble. Then I want to plant a carton of them in Joan Brockton's lab and get her implicated in the deed and maybe get her hurt some. And then I want to plant some in the Bay along the beaches around the institute."

"Jesus Christ. And where do I come in?" said Fenner.

"I am well known there and can't be seen screwing around the place, especially on campus. Plus I have a full med school schedule down here, and I'd like to get the fuck out of here on time. I need you to make the deposits, so to speak."

"So I do all the dirty work up here, take all the risk, and what's in it for me?" asked Fenner. "I don't give two shits about Brockton or the college. Having Tyson annoyed would be nice, but hardly worth what you're asking me to do."

"Name your price."

"Suggest one."

"Thousand bucks now and another when it's done successfully."

Fenner thought for a while. He could always take the grand and bail out if it looks like it is going to go badly. "Okay. What's first?"

"Okay. I'm going to ship you a carton of these jellyfish. You simply find a small lake near town that is a little secluded and dump them into it, like at night when nobody is around. But Fenner, be sure you get some of those vinyl gloves, don't touch even the water in the carton, rinse it in the lake after you're done and throw it away."

"Got it."

"Now, can your cell phone take pictures?"

"Yeah."

You need to get into Joan Brockton's lab, take pictures of one of her data notebooks, like the cover and the first few pages. You work construction, right?"

"Yep." *Christ, does this guy know what kind of toothpaste I use?*

"Wear a tool belt or something and say you are doing a routine inspection of water and gas pipes or something like that. Just be nice and act like you belong there." Griffin told Fenner where Joan's lab was. "After you pull that off, email me the pictures, and go to the campus bookstore and buy one of the same kind of notebooks she uses. Mail it to me." Griffin gave Fenner his address.

"That it?"

"No. You need to check the lake every couple of days to see if the jellies are growing there. That will be easy, because they glow in the dark, and you will see them at night. When you tell me that they are growing and causing people trouble, I will send you another carton of them and a doctored up lab notebook to put on Brockton's lab desk. You'll have to think a while about how to get in there for that. And finally, I want you to buy a bunch of bags of lawn fertilizer and start dumping them in the Boardman River as near to its mouth at the bay as you can without being seen. Night work again, bro. Start doing that now."

"Good Christ. What's the fertilizer for?"

"I want the bay to be nice and productive so the jellies have lots to eat when we make that final deposit. The institute and all of Traverse City should be in a hell of a panic by then. And if it goes right, Brockton will be arrested for it. She's well known as one of the best gene jockeys there and therefore will be a plausible perp." Griffin did not tell Fenner the part of the plan where people including Joan would be badly hurt or even killed by contacting the jellies that she would assume were the normal harmless ones.

"Alright, I guess I'll give it a shot, but you're going to have to double the money for all of that."

"Okay dude."

Fenner was now convinced that Griffin was a certifiable raving maniac. But Fenner was still going to take the money up front and see how it goes. He drove on and turned south on Garfield. He knew of a lake that should work, not far from the trailer park where he lived.

On his lunch break the next day, Fenner drove to the institute, found Joan's lab and knocked at the open door. She rose from her desk and came toward him. "Yes?"

Fenner wore a work belt full of tools and had a pressure gauge in his hand. He tried his friendliest smile. "We're doing a routine check of the gas and water plumbing system. Is this a bad time, or should I come back?"

"No, this would be fine. I was just about to go to the cafeteria for some lunch. Just be sure to close the door so that it locks when you leave."

Perfect. "Thanks ma'am."

Fenner went over to a gas line port and hooked up his pressure gauge. He fiddled with it until Joan finished at her desk and walked out of the lab, closing the door behind her. Astonished by how easy this turned out to be, Fenner waited to be sure Joan didn't come back for something she forgot, and then he went to her desk. Data notebooks were all over the top of the desk, and he picked one and pulled out his smartphone. He photographed the cover and the first few pages like Griffin had instructed him. He put the book back where it was, retrieved his pressure gauge, and left the lab. He drove the few blocks to the main campus, found the bookstore, and bought one of the notebooks that Joan and most other students and faculty used for lab notes and data. On the way home he FedExed it to Griffin and then emailed the pictures.

Two days later at Isla Colombo, Griffin labeled the cover of the new notebook the same way Joan did, and began copying his entire protocol for developing the transgenic jellyfish into the notebook with a pretty good imitation of Joan's handwriting. He FedExed a two-liter plastic container of the jellyfish and two thousand dollars in cash to Fenner.

Chapter 9

The Monday morning after Paul and Joan's weekend sail to Suttons Bay, they had a quick breakfast on Paul's boat and drove their vehicles down to the institute in Traverse. Paul went to the water analysis facility and got the toxin profile on the Whitetail Lake water and sediment samples he had brought in on Friday. There were no unusual readings. He and Joan took that report up to Dr. Casey's lab in Joan's building. They found Casey doing a necropsy on the yellow retriever.

"Poor thing," said Joan. "We heard about it yesterday from Craig Basham."

"Hi Joan," replied Casey. "Yes, I hate to see this. I'm finding the same thing I have been seeing in the otters. Mouth and nose inflammation, cerebral and pulmonary edema, and blood cytopenia. The microbiology report for the otters was negative—no evidence of infection. And as far as we know this dog's trauma, whatever it was, came on suddenly, not some chronic thing."

Paul nodded. "The water and sediment analyses were negative too, so these animals are not being poisoned by anything we are familiar with. I guess we watch and wait, for the time being. Hopefully someone will find or see something soon that will explain it. Are there any reports of this kind of thing in any of the other local lakes?"

"No. Hopefully there won't be."

Paul and Joan left Casey's lab to go to their own labs.

"I have to get the *Halcyon* ready for the southern Lake Michigan plankton cruise, which leaves on Wednesday," said Paul when they reached Joan's lab downstairs.

"Okay, see you when you get back if I don't see you before you leave. And thanks for the weekend voyage. It was very nice." She leaned and gave Paul a kiss, and entered her lab.

Paul went next door to the limnology building. Several student technicians were already pushing carts loaded with cases of sample bottles and other supplies out to the ship at her dockside mooring. Paul boarded the *Halcyon* to supervise the activities. He would be the chief scientist for this cruise, and was no longer expected to do a lot of the loading work himself like he had done when he had been a grad student. He went up to the bridge to check the float plan with Captain Robado, the short, stocky, always affable skipper of the *Halcyon*. The locations of the sampling transects were the same as had been done in previous cruises, and there was nothing other than the sailing dates to confirm.

"Departure Wednesday at oh nine hundred, return from Chicago Saturday morning?" Robado queried.

"That's the gig," replied Paul. He glanced out of the pilothouse window before leaving, and noticed that the water in the harbor was greener and less transparent than usual. "Did you notice the water, Cap?"

Robado looked out the window. "Yeah, but I figure that's your department. I just drive this tub wherever you want to go."

Paul smiled and went down the stairs and out on the dock. He walked out to the end of the dock, and was stunned at the sight of a phytoplankton bloom like he had never seen on the Bay. It seemed to be hugging the shore in a band fifteen or twenty meters wide. *Holy mackerel, when and why did this happen?* Paul went into the headquarters office in the limnology building and found David Washington, the marine superintendent at the institute.

"Dave, can I take the *Chinook* out for an hour or so? I need to get some samples to find out what is going on with a plankton bloom right here along the shoreline."

Washington checked the ship-time schedule and saw that *Chinook* was not scheduled for use for the next several days. "Sure Paul. Do you need help?"

"I'll see if I can get the new kid in our lab. Thanks Dave."

Paul went down the hall to his lab. Dr. Perry was there chatting with Brad Barlow about Barlow's research project that was part of his rotation in Perry's lab.

"Hi Dr. Perry, Brad. Glad you're both here. I've just noticed a hell of an algal bloom just offshore here. I've never seen one like it in the bay. I want to get out there and get some samples. Can you spare an hour, Brad, to help me take the *Chinook* out to do that?"

"Sure," said Brad.

"I think I'll tag along," said Perry. "I haven't been out on *Chinook* in a long time."

Paul gathered a Van Dorn water sampler, the Wisconsin plankton net, and some plastic sample bottles, and the three of them went out to the harbor. The *Chinook* was moored at her usual berth on the east side of the rectangular harbor across from the *Halcyon*. They went aboard with the equipment, and Paul started the diesel engine. While it was warming up he expressed a pet peeve of his.

"You know something that bugs me? So many of the novels I read involving boats are written by authors who obviously are not boaters—the characters always seem to jump in the boat, cast off the lines and only then start up the engine. What if the engine won't start and you drift away from the dock? Like today, this east wind would have us crashing over into the *Halcyon* in no time. C'mon man, you start it first, *then* cast off!"

"Yeah, I've come across that a time or two myself," replied Perry. "Well Brad, I guess Captain Tyson would allow you to get on the dock and release the lines now; the temperature gauge is coming up."

Brad took the lines off of the cleats, threw them to Paul and Perry and then stepped back aboard. Paul backed the 35-foot boat away from the dock and took her out through the harbor entrance with a warning blast from the horn. He drove the boat slowly out to just beyond the edge of the plankton bloom, and then cruised slowly back and forth along the bloom to get a sense of how far it extended in each direction.

"This thing seems to be generally centered around the mouth of the Boardman River, and the bloom seems densest there. My god, it looks so much like split pea soup that you could probably pull chunks of ham out of it with a spoon. Let's get some samples all along it."

Paul made five sampling stops, one at the river and two to each side of it at 100-meter intervals. At each location they filled a sample bottle with water taken by the Van Dorn sampler and another bottle with water containing the concentrate from the plankton net sample. They motored back to the RULI harbor, moored and secured the boat, and returned to the limnology building. Brad and Perry took the equipment and the plankton samples to the lab, while Paul returned the boat keys to the main office and took the water samples to the water analysis facility.

"We need a full nutrient profile on these samples ASAP. There's a hell of a bloom right out front. Can you work these in to your schedule?"

"Yes," said the lab tech. "We're not too busy right now. Probably have the results available tomorrow."

"Super," replied Paul. He walked back to the Perry lab, and found Perry and Brad chatting again while they looked at the plankton samples they had just taken.

"It's a classic bloom of diatoms and green algae. The water's still a little cold for bluegreens, but they'll be along soon," said Perry. "Earlier this morning Brad and I had been kicking around ideas for his term project. We've just agreed that it would be timely for him to investigate this bloom."

"Great idea," said Paul. "I'd jump on it myself, but I've got the *Halcyon* cruise this week."

They continued to discuss the approach that Brad should take. Because the Boardman River already looked suspicious as the source of nutrient loading for the bloom, they agreed that Brad should plan to take a series of river water samples from the mouth back upriver for a couple of miles or so to see if there is a nearby point source. Dr. Perry went back to his office to continue reviewing grant proposals for the National Science Foundation, and Paul went to his desk in the lab to continue working on a manuscript for publication. Before getting to work he decided to call Craig Basham.

"Craig, we have a very unusual plankton bloom here at the foot of West Bay. I'm suspicious of nutrient loading from the Boardman. There hasn't been a major problem in the river for quite some time. You might want to keep your ears open; we will be sampling to see if we can detect a point source, but it might be something broader than that."

"Christ, never a dull moment," replied Craig. "Any dead animals floating around out there?"

"No no, nothing like that. Not related to the Whitetail Lake thing." Paul paused a moment. "At least not as far as we can tell right now."

"Okay, thanks Paul. Keep me informed about the sampling results."

"Will do."

Paul booted up his computer for the manuscript work.

Chapter 10

On the same morning that the West Bay plankton bloom samples were being taken in Traverse City, Juanita Salazar was busy down in Isla Colombo. She had had a sleepless night after Griffin had brutally humiliated her. She was frightened of him now, so much so that she called in for a sick-leave day and started looking for a new apartment. She also changed her telephone number. If there had been any other nursing jobs available on the island she would have applied for that too. As it was, from now on she would have to avoid Griffin as much as possible at the med school, maybe by going in to her infirmary job very early, bringing her lunch with her, and leaving very late. She was also frightened by her own anger at him that was reaching an intensity that was causing thoughts of retaliatory acts that went against her devout Catholicism. And above all, she was angry at herself for having had such naïve hopes that he would be the shining knight who would fall in love with her and carry her off to a blissful life in the U.S., hopes that had been shattered among the shards of her diploma frame glass on the floor around her yesterday.

It was bad enough that she had sinned by sleeping with him unwed. She had confessed this to her priest some time ago, and Griffin was the only man she had done this with, but she had not stopped this behavior. She would stop now of course, and she wanted that to be the end of it. She wanted to tell her brother Luis, if only to seek his protection from

Griffin, but she was afraid of what Luis would think of her and of what he might attempt do to Griffin that would land him in jail or worse.

Juanita, who was now 27, had gone to college and nursing school on St. Thomas with funding from an Isla Colombo scholarship program for increasing the numbers of professional native citizens. She had been one of the program's success stories, but she in fact harbored the ambition to seek a career in the U.S., the unfortunate risk for third world countries attempting to get their people educated abroad. Her brother had not gone to college, but had become a successful charter fishing boat captain and now operated his own boat. Their parents were no longer living, and all they had was their mixed, or mestizo, heritage of Spanish, West Indian, and African ancestors. She was proud of that and hated the way Griffin had spat the word mestiza at her like it was a scatalogical epithet.

Juanita drove around to visit several apartments that were available; the economy was not so good and vacancies were numerous. Shortly after noon she found one that she liked and wrote a check immediately for the deposit and first month's rent. It was small but nice, and it was just two blocks from the waterfront where visiting her brother would be a short walk. She walked there now, and entered the marina gateway after showing her ID at the customs and immigration checkpoint. The St. Thomas ferry docked here, and Isla Colombo was fussy about who came and went through its sea and air portals.

Out on the docks she found Luis eating a taco in the aft cockpit of his boat in his slip at the marina. It was an old 1992 Bertram 28 flybridge cruiser that he had bought cheap at a repo sale. Bathed in the Caribbean sun, 30-year-old Luis was young-looking at five feet six with short black hair and a blinding white smile. Shirtless in khaki cargo shorts and flip flops, he waved from his seat in the fighting chair.

"Juanita! Cómo estás?" Luis got up and came to the boarding plank. He continued in Spanish, "Can I make you some lunch? Why are you here and not working?"

Juanita had to think fast for an explanation. She settled on the truth, for now. "I was looking for a new apartment, and I have found one near here."

"Come aboard and tell me why you are moving, while I make you a taco."

She walked aboard and followed Luis into the galley just forward of the cockpit.

"I don't like the one I have been in." Still true.

"I thought it was pretty nice."

"It was, but the new manager is not good and is talking about raising the rent." So much for the truth. "Luis, could you help me move? Are you free today?"

"I am free, and of course I will help you. But why so suddenly? Something is going on, Juanita. I am your brother; I see it in your eyes."

Her troubled gaze fell to the deck, and she was silent. They ate the tacos and drank some papaya juice, and Luis put on a tee shirt and some boat shoes. He locked up the boat and they walked to the marina gate where the officials waved them through, having just seen Juanita's ID and recognizing Luis as a regular at the marina. They went to his car, drove to Juanita's car, and he followed her to her old apartment.

At the old apartment they packed up Juanita's things, which all fit into the two small cars; all of the furniture belonged to the apartment. On the last trip through the apartment Luis's shoe crunched on some of the broken glass Juanita had missed when cleaning up near the desk that morning. He looked at her with raised eyebrows.

"I dropped a juice glass this morning. Lucky it was empty." More lies. Eyes toward the floor.

"Tell me Juanita."

"Please Luis. It is over. There is nothing to talk about now. Let's go, please."

"You come to me if you need me. Promise."

"Of course, Luis."

She gave him her new phone number, and he nodded slowly. He started to question her again, but she stopped him with a finger pressed firmly to his lips and led him quickly out to their cars. They drove to the new apartment and got the stuff moved in within an hour. Luis made her promise again to call immediately if something went wrong, and left to return to his boat. He had a client scheduled for the following morning.

Juanita put away some of her things and then got online on her computer. She updated her resume and emailed it to every hospital, urgent care clinic, nursing home, and school with a first aid room in St. Croix, St. Thomas, and Puerto Rico.

CHAPTER 11

The next day Juanita got up early, ate breakfast quickly, packed a sandwich and fruit lunch, and drove to work at the medical campus infirmary hoping to avoid seeing Griffin. She was successful only until the middle of that afternoon.

In Dr. Mendoza's lab, a custodial employee was preparing to sweep the floor when he noticed a small wet blob of something lying on the floor and bent to pick it up. Griffin realized too late that he had dropped one of his jellyfish from his transfer net, and shouted just as the young man grabbed it with his bare hand. The man screamed in pain and started staggering around trying to shake it off of his hand. Griffin, who wore vinyl gloves, pulled the jellyfish off the man's hand and poured some acetic acid on the hand. Acetic acid was kept in ready supply for just such an accident, as it inhibits the firing of the stinger cells.

But stingers that had already fired had done their damage, and the man's trauma worsened, and Griffin shouted for Dr. Mendoza. Mendoza came out of his office, took one look, and rushed back into his office for a dose of box jelly antidote that he kept for emergencies. He gave the custodian an injection, but it was slow to take effect, and the man remained in trouble. Dr. Mendoza and Griffin got the nearly unconscious man onto a lab cart and wheeled him out of the building and over to the infirmary.

Juanita stiffened when she saw them wheel the young man into the emergency room. She avoided Griffin's eyes as Dr. Mendoza spoke to him.
"I will supervise Carlos's treatment here. I want you to go back to the lab and post some big signs warning everyone not to touch those animals. That really should have already been done."
Griffin nodded and left the room.
"What happened?" asked Juanita.
"This man tried to pick up one of Mr. Griffin's jellyfish and got stung."
"Oh. Larry works with jellyfish?" Juanita was amazed to hear that, remembering Griffin's near fatal encounter.
"Yes."
"But this is a small exposure just to the hand; it shouldn't be serious."
"Except this was a special case. This was one of the freshwater jellyfish that Mr. Griffin has made transgenic with box jelly toxin genes. One of the most lethal combinations of toxins in the world. The first time this has been done with freshwater jellies."
"Oh my," said Juanita. "Why is he doing that?"
"It is a term project for my gene technology course. But Mr. Griffin needs to be more careful. And we need to keep quiet about this incident." Dr. Mendoza looked at her sternly. "Can you do that, Ms. Salazar?"
"Yes sir."
They got the man hooked up to a heart and blood pressure monitor and administered a pain medication in an IV drip. The man seemed to be responding to the antidote and was breathing quietly.
Juanita hoped that Griffin would not come back to the infirmary.

CHAPTER 12

On Tuesday morning Brad Barlow got started with his sampling of the water in the Boardman River. The day was sunny and warm with little wind. He loaded a box of one-liter plastic bottles in the institute's 12-foot flat-bottom john boat with a ten-horse outboard and ran the boat over to the mouth of the river. Just inside the river mouth he filled a sample bottle at the surface of the water, turned on the lab's hand-held GPS unit, and ran the boat two tenths of a mile upstream for the next sample. The plan was to sample every two tenths of a mile as he wound his way upstream through Traverse City.

Right away Brad noticed masses of filamentous algae, especially along shore. He did not know what they were or whether it was normal for them to be there, but he kept his eye on them as he continued his sampling until it was time for a brief lunch break. He pulled to the side of the river, tied on to a dock piling, and pulled out a sandwich from his backpack.

A few miles away, Jerry Fenner also stopped work for his lunch break and drove to a McDonald's. Sitting in his truck at the parking lot he made a call to Larry Griffin in Isla Colombo, who answered immediately.

"This is Griffin."
"Things are happening."
"This Jerry?"

"Yeah. Animals are dying in the lake."

"Like what?"

"A bunch of muskrats or some damn thing, and then somebody's mutt. Actually a kid's yellow lab. Stirring up quite a fuss."

"Good. Do they know what is causing it?"

"Don't seem to."

"They'll figure it out pretty soon, and pretty soon some people are going to get hurt. I think it's time to send you another carton to slip onto Joan Brockton's desk."

"How bad are these people gonna get hurt? Those fuckin' animals are *dead*, man."

"Oh, just bad enough to cause some real panic and get Brockton in a world of trouble. In addition to the new carton of jellyfish, I'm sending you the lab notebook to put on her desk. If you can, look in her desk for a comb or hairbrush, and try to grab some strands of her hair and scatter them in the notebook. I'm also sending an anonymous note to mail to the cops to suggest searching her lab. By the way, I assume you won't get your fingerprints on any of this shit."

Fenner was silent for a beat. "I'm not real thrilled with all of this."

"Hey, it's working just great. How is the plankton bloom coming in the bay?"

"Pretty thick now."

"Well, keep pouring in the fertilizer."

"Okay. But I'm gettin' nervous."

"I'll throw in an extra thou with the stuff I'm sending."

"That will help."

They ended the call, and Fenner drove back to the worksite.

After Brad Barlow finished his lunch he continued his sampling run in the Boardman River. After he sampled the water at the place where Eighth Street crossed the river, he noticed that the filamentous algal masses were no longer present upstream from there. He continued sampling until he reached Boardman Lake. On his way back downstream, he collected some of the filamentous algae below Eighth Street to show Paul and Dr. Perry.

At 4:30 p.m. Paul had just returned to the lab from a *Halcyon* cruise meeting when Brad walked in with his samples. He set the crate of plastic bottles down on the lab bench near Paul's desk.

"Here they are, one every two-tenths mile upstream from the mouth; each site is marked in the GPS."

"Good. How far upstream did you get?"

"Up to Boardman Lake. I think I already know where a point source is for nutrient loading. I think it is where Eighth Street crosses the river. All along the river from the mouth to Eighth I was noticing a lot of algae mats near shore, and they stopped just downstream of where Eighth Street crosses the river. I went on upstream beyond that point to get samples all the way to Boardman Lake, but I think they will show no nutrient elevations compared to the ones from Eighth Street on down. And there's no big bloom in Boardman Lake. These are the algae I found." Brad handed Paul a plastic sandwich bag with a gob of algae in it.

"Looks like *Cladophora*. They grow fast in nutrient rich water." Paul put some under a microscope. "Yep, it's *Cladophora*. Good work. We'll get these water samples analyzed, but in the meantime, I'm going to call Craig Basham and suggest we try to arrange some kind of surveillance of that site at Eighth Street. Maybe you could help with that. Feel like doing some detective work?"

"Hell yeah," said Brad.

Paul dialed Craig. "Hey big guy, I think we have a trail to the nutrient loading causing the algae bloom on the bay. Can you get over here to the lab?"

"Anything to get away from paperwork for a while," replied Basham. "See you in a few."

Paul took the water samples down the hall to the water analysis lab, and learned that his samples taken yesterday from the bay front showed maximum phosphate and nitrate concentrations at the river mouth, as he had expected. When he got back to the lab he could see through the windows that Craig Basham's Ford Escape was pulling into the parking lot. Basham unlimbered out of the vehicle and lumbered across the lot toward the building. Paul turned to his computer and pulled up a Google satellite image of Traverse City focused on the Boardman River from the mouth to Boardman Lake. Craig Basham entered the lab, and Paul introduced them to each other.

"Craig, this is Brad Barlow, rotating in our lab this summer. Brad, this is Craig Basham, the fiercest environmental attorney on the planet. You don't want him catching you even spitting in a mud puddle."

"Pleased to meet you, Brad," said Craig shaking Brad's hand and eying his spiked hair and earrings. Brad nodded.

"Craig, Brad has done some good work sampling the river water and was smart enough to notice where a bunch of *Cladophora* are growing." Paul showed Craig the bag of algae. "Look on the computer here. The algae are abundant all the way from Eighth Street here down to the mouth, but none upstream of Eighth. The water samples are being analyzed now, but dollars to donuts the phosphates and nitrates will be high from there on down; they're definitely high in the bay at the mouth—we know that already."

"Looks like a point source all right; kind of a weird place for it. There's no construction going on near there that I know of, but we can check that out. It looks like there is a public parking lot right next to the river there on the north side of Eighth Street."

"Yes, there is." replied Brad.

"Craig, you're the expert at smoking out polluters," said Paul. "I want to help, but I have to go to sea tomorrow for the rest of the week. Brad here is available though, so what do you want to do?"

"First we need to get over to that site and look around. Then we can decide what to do. Brad, can you come with me now to take a look?"

"Sure," replied Brad.

Paul thought a minute, and said, "I've got some time right now too, so I think I'll tag along."

"Okay," said Craig. "Let's go."

Ten minutes later the three of them got out of Craig's Escape in the parking lot at Eighth Street and walked to the line of trees along the river. Looking down at the water they could see the *Cladophora* mats hugging the shore of the river. They walked upstream toward the Eighth Street bridge, and saw that there were no mats under it and upstream of it. They turned back around and followed the river along the parking lot. Halfway along the lot Brad spied a large crumpled paper sack lying against a tree.

"Look at this," said Brad as he straightened out the sack. It was an empty 20-pound bag of lawn fertilizer.

"Odd place for that," said Craig. He stepped over to the edge of the river and looked at the ground. "Looks like some spilled fertilizer granules right here. Like it was getting dumped in the river. Why would someone do that?"

"Somebody getting rid of some extra he didn't need maybe?" said Paul.

"I suppose," replied Craig. "Whatever, they must have been doing it more than once for all the eutrophication that is going on clear out into the bay. And it needs to stop. We need to start watching this place, especially at night. It's likely whoever is doing it knows it's not kosher to do it. Brad, give me your phone number, and I'll organize a few people I know who will be willing to do some surveillance with us on a rotating basis. Hopefully we can catch someone in the act."

Brad gave Craig his cell number and the lab number, and Craig drove Brad and Paul back to the institute.

CHAPTER 13

Seagulls shrieked up off the institute's dock pilings as the long blast of *Halcyon's* horn signaled her departure from the harbor for the plankton cruise on Lake Michigan. It was 8 a.m. Wednesday, the sky was clear with a few high cirrus clouds, and the 8-knot northwest wind had flags rippling lazily. From the fantail Paul waved to Joan, who waved back. Joan watched the ship pass slowly through the harbor mouth and stand northward out into the sparkling blue West Bay. She waved once again and then turned back up the dock toward her lab to get a grip before her teaching day started; she had two three-hour intro bio labs ahead of her.

On the *Halcyon* Paul got busy in his role of chief scientist for this cruise and immediately organized the technical team of grad students and undergrads for the task of getting the sampling equipment ready for the first sampling station. The new assistant professor, Carol Martin, was aboard as well. Dr. Martin was a tall, attractive brunette who was studious but congenial with an enthusiastic smile. She was primarily just observing the activities; normally a professor would be the chief scientist rather than a postdoc like Paul, but Martin had only recently arrived on campus after being recruited from her postdoc position at the University of Minnesota, and was not fully familiar with the institute's cruise protocol and its oceanographic-scale instrumentation and methodology. In fact, Martin was actually younger than Paul, and Paul had over six years of experience on *Halcyon* cruises. But Paul knew of Martin's research in zooplankton ecology, and knew that it was first rate and that Martin would make the transition from small lakes to the Great Lakes rapidly. Paul was also pleased that the institute had finally managed to attract an excellent replacement for the disgraced former assistant professor Eldon Bates, who was involved in the scandalous plagiarism of Paul's work that had cost the life of Bates' graduate student Ronald Withers. It was Withers' fatal injury on the *Halcyon* that Paul had nearly been convicted of causing two years ago.

Paul and the students assembled the rosette of twelve 20-liter gray plastic Niskin water samplers on the cylindrical stainless-steel frame and attached the cable that served both as hoisting support and electronic communication with the sampler array and accompanying sensors. They tested the computer controls of the closure releases of each Niskin bottle, checked the function of the underwater light meter, and calibrated the multiparameter water quality monitor that sent the shipboard computer the data on depth, temperature, pH, conductivity, alkalinity (convertible to carbon dioxide content), turbidity, and total algal chlorophyll content. All systems were working perfectly. They then labeled the plastic sample bottles that would receive the samples from the Niskin bottles and filled out the data sheet for the first sampling station. That left them with a couple of hours to relax and enjoy the ride until they cleared the mouth of Traverse Bay and reached station 1 a few miles to the west in northern Lake Michigan.

When the *Halcyon* passed north of Lighthouse Point at the tip of the Leelanau Peninsula into open Lake Michigan, wave action increased from the moderate northwest wind. Sitting in his favorite resting spot up on the lifeboat deck, Paul felt the increased rolling motion and was painfully reminded that this was the location two years ago when Ron Withers was bashed in the head by a heavy hatch cover that was thrown over on him down in a storage hold while the *Halcyon* was rolling violently in the rising windstorm that day.

The *Halcyon* turned westward, and an hour later was passing to the north of Manitou Island. This was where, two years ago, Paul was escorted by the mate and chief engineer down from the boat deck to the wardroom under suspicion of being responsible for Ron Wither's apparent disappearance from the ship. Paul now found himself reliving the rest of that nightmarish day, when they finally found Withers mortally injured in the hold and suspected Paul of carrying out the threat that Paul had recklessly and publicly made to Withers earlier when Paul had discovered Wither's plagiarism of Paul's data. Paul had been up here on the boat deck the whole time Withers was below in the hold, but no one could verify that except Withers' mentor Dr. Bates, who kept silent until the last moment in Paul's murder trial. Bates had crumbled on the witness stand when confronted with his extensive plagiarism that Paul and Joan had discovered by online comparisons of his publications with others.

Paul now winced at the memory of the worst part of the whole sordid affair, when his out-of-control anger over the whole thing got him estranged from Joan; he had lost his temper when she asked for reassurance that he had not attacked Withers. The two weeks of their estrangement seemed like forever, until she herself discovered that Withers' injury had been an accident caused by the hatch cover. In the meantime Joan had gone out with Larry Griffin a couple of times and nearly been raped by him. Despite Joan's discovery of how the accident had happened, the prosecutor had chosen to continue the case against Paul with the theory that Paul had thrown the hatch cover down on Withers. To make matters worse, Larry Griffin carried out his threat to Joan that he would falsely testify that he saw Paul go below while Withers was missing. Only Dr. Bates' admission that he could see Paul up on deck the whole time saved Paul from going to prison for life.

Wondering again where that son of a bitch Griffin was now and what he was up to, Paul was mercifully brought out of his unpleasant reverie by the loud ring of the bridge signal to the engine room to slow and stop the ship. They were arriving at sampling station 1. He got up and went forward to the bridge and descended the stairs to main deck level.

As the ship slowed to a stop, three student techs wearing bright orange life vests manhandled the heavy sampling rosette out onto the "hero board," the steel grate platform extending from the port side of the foredeck out over the water. The slack in the cable was taken in by the winch operator. When the ship was fully stopped and gently rolling in the trough broadside to the light wind, Captain Robado nodded from an open bridge window. The winch operator slowly lifted the rosette above the railing of the hero board and one of the techs eased the cable out over the water. The tubular stainless steel rosette frame glinted brightly in the sun as it slowly sank into the water. All of the Niskin bottles were set in their open configuration, allowing water to freely course through them.

As the equipment descended through the water column, Paul watched the deck monitor for the readout of water conditions relayed by the underwater sensors. He was paying special attention to the temperature and light levels. He wanted to know where the thermocline was, which was the depth at which the water temperature rapidly became colder than the warm upper layer. And he wanted to know when the equipment had reached the depth where the photosynthetically available light radiation (PAR) was reduced to 1% of the surface light.

At the 1% light depth Paul signaled the winch operator to halt the descent of the rosette frame. He then pushed the switches that sent the electronic signal to close the first three Niskin bottles, capturing water at that depth.

"There's your main zooplankton community," Paul said to Dr. Martin, who nodded with a smile. Zooplankton migrate down out of the light during the day, perhaps to avoid predation, though no one knows for sure the evolutionary and ecological basis for this strong behavior pattern.

"Start it back up, Megan," Paul said to the young woman operating the winch. The days of male-only marine research were long in the past.

When the deck readout indicated that the rosette was reentering the thermocline, Paul signaled for a halt again and closed the next three Niskin bottles. Phytoplankton tended to accumulate there where the cold-water density was higher, as the algae slowly sink down from the upper water column. He got another three samples halfway between the thermocline and the surface, and the final three at the surface. The equipment was carefully winched up onto the hero board and carried to its stand on the foredeck. The sampling cast had taken only 20 minutes, and as the Captain got the *Halcyon* underway on a southwesterly course toward Manitowok, Wisconsin, the "rosette dance" began.

A parade of student techs began slowly circling the rosette, opening the Niskin spigots to fill sample bottles labeled according to the depth and replicate number. The three Niskin samplers at a given depth provided triplicate samples from that depth, essential for meaningful statistics. For the phytoplankton work, one liter from each Niskin sampler was drawn and treated with an iodine preservative solution. The remaining 19 liters in each Niskin bottle were passed through a wide-mouth funnel with a zooplankton-net-mesh at its neck, and the concentrated zooplankton sample was rinsed into a sample bottle and given an ethanol preservative solution. All of the water quality data from the underwater sensors were automatically logged in the deck receiver unit; these data were backed up by downloading them into the computer.

As the *Halcyon* steamed on toward station 2, the Niskin samplers were rinsed with fresh water and re-cocked to their open positions, and a new set of sample bottles were labeled. That left over an hour to go the rest of the 20 miles to station 2, and everyone relaxed in the sun and told lies and bad jokes. It was all the young students could do to assuage their suffering from being out of cell phone range and thus cut off from their habitual texting and net surfing. Paul thought he could see their thumbs still reflexively drumming on imaginary keypads.

The beautiful weather continued the rest of the day as the scientific crew rattled off the four additional stations leading into Manitowok, where the relieved students could pull out their smartphones and get back to thumbing on them. The old cook, "Tiny" Palatine, who was anything but tiny, had served a sumptuous if carbo-heavy dinner in the wardroom well before the *Halcyon* tied up at the city coal dock at 8:15 p.m., and most of the ship's company headed straight for the waterfront bars and their cheap draft beer. Paul, Carol Martin, and the senior officers returned to the ship after just a couple, but everyone else stayed for more and would suffer for it the next morning.

CHAPTER 14

The quiet air at 7 a.m. on Thursday was shattered as Tiny the cook began banging two pots together at the head of the ladder to the forecastle, where all the students' bunks were. "DROP YOUR COCKS AND GRAB YOUR SOCKS AND GET YOUR ASSES UP TO BREAKFAST," Tiny hollered as though this was a navy ship in 1944. Paul, Carol Martin and Captain Robado could hear it clear back in the wardroom, and they all shook their heads.

"The old coot keeps forgetting that half the kids in the foc'sle are women," said Robado. "I swear he's going to get us all fired for sexual harassment—him and me at least."

"Does he talk like that often?" asked Martin.

"Mostly an occasional ribald joke," said Paul. "But as far as I can tell, most of the women think he's a comical old anachronism and essentially harmless, and they don't seem to feel threatened by him. But he is eventually going to really piss someone off, and he needs to be warned to knock it off." Paul looked at the captain. "Isn't he going to retire soon?"

"I wish," replied Robado. "But I can't push him—he does know enough to sue for age discrimination. Anyway, I'll talk to him later today. I'll warn him that *I'll* file sexual harassment charges on the ladies' behalf, though I don't know if it can be done that way."

The conversation ended as students began straggling into the wardroom with noticeable hangovers. The captain went up to the bridge to get the *Halcyon* underway for the day's run southeastward to Grand Haven, Michigan, with another five sampling stations scheduled on that course.

Some clouds had moved in overnight and the wind was a bit stronger than yesterday, but conditions were still good for working over the side, and the sampling stations went smoothly and on schedule. Dr. Martin began doing some of the computer control of the rosette samplers, and Paul's prediction that she would pick it up fast was right on the money. At 5:30 p.m. the final sampling cast was pulled out of the water a few miles off the breakwaters of Grand Haven, and Captain Robado rang the chief engineer to start the engine and gave the helmsman the course for the Grand Haven breakwaters.

Also at 5:30 up in Traverse City, Jerry Fenner arrived home from work and found the expected FedEx package on the doorstep of his trailer. He brought the box into the trailer, got a beer out of the mini fridge, and opened the package.

Without touching anything inside the box, Fenner noted that there was a familiar plastic tub with the Baines Biological Supply logo on the lid and the stick-on label showing the species name of the freshwater jellyfish, *Craspedacusta sowerbyi,* that Fenner couldn't begin to pronounce. Also in the box was the lab notebook that he had sent to Griffin, and a sealed envelope addressed to the county sheriff with a Post-it note attached that said "mail this the day before you put the carton on Brockton's desk." That got Fenner feeling nervous again. He put on a pair of the vinyl gloves he had bought and pulled the notebook out of the box. It now had Joan Brockton's name handwritten on the cover. He leafed through it, saw what to him was a bunch of gibberish, and put it back in the box.

Fenner closed the box, made a thick Spam sandwich, and turned on the TV. He nodded as he listened to someone on Fox News ranting about the goddamn liberals, and he forgot about the box for a while.

In Grand Haven that evening, Paul skipped the bar-hopping and called Joan from his chief scientist stateroom on the bridge deck of the *Halcyon*.

"Hi Paul, where are you and how goes it?"

"Grand Haven. It's going very well. Carol Martin's already got the hang of the routine; she'll be chief scientist next cruise no problem."

"Good for her."

"How about you?"

"Yesterday was my teaching day, pretty much the normal routine. It takes longer and longer to get them to quit texting and shut off their phones to get the class started."

"I know what you mean. You should see the kids out here when we are out of cell phone range. They need methadone for the withdrawal symptoms."

"Exactly. Well, I had a pretty productive day in the lab today. My genes are working well—correction, my Coho salmon's genes are working well. I wi…"

"Your genes are just fine too, babe," Paul interrupted.

"Oh shush. Anyway, I was about to say that tomorrow I will be over at the fish hatchery to help with their operations and get some more fingerlings. I'll probably be home late, and then in to my lab early on Saturday."

"Okay. We will make the transect from here over to Chicago tomorrow, and start back up the lake on Saturday."

"Sounds good. Miss you."

"You too. Bye Joanie."

Paul went out on deck to watch the fountain and light show that Grand Haven puts on every summer night alongside the harbor channel.

CHAPTER 15

At 7 a.m. on Friday morning Joan rose out of bed, shut off her alarm clock and got a glass of orange juice from the fridge, which was only a few steps away from her day bed in the small studio apartment. She put on some old jeans and a work shirt for her day at the state fish hatchery over on the Platte River near Lake Michigan, where she volunteered now and then in return for access to their Coho salmon juveniles that she used in her research. She enjoyed her view of West Bay as she sat at her little table and ate a quick breakfast. It was sunny and breezy out there, and a boat was slowly making its way northward with two downriggers set at the stern rail for trolling. Joan finished up, rinsed her dishes, and went downstairs to her Blazer. She drove the few blocks to the lab to do a couple of things before the trip to the hatchery.

"Hi Amanda," Joan said as she went through the open lab door.

"Hi Joan," replied the young woman in a white lab coat as she worked at the sink cleaning glassware. Slender and attractive with straight black hair, Amanda was a sophomore student assistant on hourly wages to help with her college expenses.

Joan straightened out some of the equipment on her lab bench, checked to make sure the water in her fish tanks was at the right temperature and circulating properly, and grabbed a ten-gallon plastic bucket for the new juveniles she would get at the hatchery.

"I'll be over at the hatchery all day, and will be back late," Joan said to Amanda.

"Okay. Have a good one."

"Thanks. Be sure to lock up when you leave."

"Oh yes," replied Amanda.

As Joan pulled out of the institute parking lot, a white F150 pickup passed her on its way into the lot. She was startled into a the vivid memory of Jake Fenner's battered old truck as it barreled down the lot and out on the dock toward her and Paul two years ago. She shook her head and drove on. *I gotta quit being spooked by every damn white pickup I see.*

Jerry Fenner parked his truck, picked up the FedEx box and walked to Joan's building. He was dressed in clean work clothes and wore his tool belt like he had the last time he was here. Arriving at Joan's lab, he found the door open. *So far, so good.* He knocked and waited a moment.

"Yes?" said the attractive young lady who appeared at the door.

"Excuse me miss. I'm here to finish some work on the gas spigots. I was here last week; another lady was here then."

"Oh that must have been Joan. She's away at the fish hatchery today."

Perfect. Fenner nodded and showed her the box. "This is a new gas spigot. Are you using the gas right now?"

"No I'm just washing glassware. Go ahead."

"Thanks sweetie." Amanda reddened slightly at that unwelcome comment and turned quickly back toward the sink.

Fenner carried the box to the lab bench near Joan's desk and began clanking at a gas spigot with one of his wrenches. When he was sure the girl was engrossed in her work at the sink with her back to him, he opened the box and quickly put the jellyfish tub on Joan's desk. He looked at Amanda again to make sure her back was still toward him, and quietly pulled open the desk drawer. Griffin had guessed right— there was a hairbrush in there, and Fenner pulled off a few strands of hair and slid them between a couple pages of the notebook Griffin had sent him. He put the notebook under some others that were on the desk. He was wearing work gloves to keep his fingerprints off the tub and the notebook. Back at the bench he clanked on the gas pipes some more and revved his battery-powered drill a few times, and then holstered the tools, grabbed the empty box and headed for the door.

"Thanks again sweetie."

Amanda ignored him and kept working.

CHAPTER 16

Later that morning the *Halcyon* was at the second sampling station of the day, forty miles southwest of Grand Haven. When Paul and the crew finished getting the equipment back aboard, Captain Robado leaned out of the open window on the bridge.

"Paul, could you come up here when you have a minute?"

"Sure Cap. Be right there." He finished downloading the sensor data into the computer and went up to the bridge.

"We have a problem with the radar," Robado said. "About fifteen minutes ago it just flat quit, and we have no idea why. We have located a marine service facility on the Chicago River that can work on it tomorrow. That will delay the schedule hopefully by just one day. But we shouldn't continue after today without radar. Fortunately there is no rain or fog in the forecast for now."

"That sounds okay."

"Okay, except we will have to go through five drawbridges and disrupt the hell out of Chicago traffic this evening. That will be a hoot."

"Jeez. They'll love us. Well, let me know if I can help in any way."

"Thanks Paul."

Paul went down to join Carol Martin for a coffee. He told her about the repair situation and asked if the delay will be a problem for her.

"No, my husband can handle the kids for another day. I'll just lose a day of grant writing, which I frankly won't miss."

"How is that going?"

"Pretty well. By the way, my work has a global warming component, like yours does. I've been wondering when the political imbroglio over global warming is going to impact the availability of federal funding for research on that subject. I can see the potential for a ban on that coming like the one that was placed on federal funding for embryonic stem cell research, depending on who has or gets hold of the reins in Washington."

"Lord, what a thought. You might have something there—I guess there's no end to the foolishness down there." Paul took a sip of coffee and they lapsed into contemplative silence as the chuffeta-chuffeta-chuffeta of the old twelve-cylinder diesel engine droned on.

After three more sampling stations the *Halcyon* was approaching Chicago, the great skyline backlit by the late afternoon sun. A number of sailboats were out in the perfect sailing conditions, a good 12 knot west wind with nearly flat water in the lee of the land. Captain Robado brought the ship slowly into the mouth of the Chicago River. He had radioed the harbormaster about his need to bring the ship to the marine facility between State and Dearborn streets, and the bridge operators had all been alerted. At dead slow the *Halcyon* proceeded smoothly through the drawbridges at Lake Shore Drive, Columbus Drive, Michigan Avenue, and Wabash Avenue, the bridges going up and back down sequentially in a choreographed ballet.

Then all hell broke loose. After opening part way, the State Street bridge got stuck. There was no way for the *Halcyon* to get by, and the Wabash bridge had already closed behind them with traffic streaming over it again.

"Jesus Christ," barked Robado as he leaped for the command signal telegraph and almost yanked off the handles ringing for full astern. The chief engineer was standing by in the engine room knowing that maneuvers were coming soon, but *full* astern was a surprise. He gave it to Robado as fast as he could, and stood on full alert for the next command while the propeller cavitated in its attempt to gain reverse thrust and the big drive shaft began shaking violently.

Up on deck everyone watched in horror as they approached the stuck bridge, the ship shuddering like a semi with its brakes locked up. It didn't look like the ship would stop in time. "GET BACK OFF THE FOREDECK," Robado hollered out the window at the deckhands and scientific staff, who all ran back along the covered side decks aft of the face of the pilothouse. The ship finally came to a halt with the forward mast hovering within feet of the bridge. Robado rang for slow astern and wiped a torrent of sweat from his forehead. The ship slowly backed away from the bridge, but the problems had only begun. The closed Wabash bridge was less than a ship's length behind them, and the Venturi Effect in the canyon of tall buildings had the west wind funneling down the river at 20 knots.

To make matters worse, single screw boats like the *Halcyon* were impossible to back up in a straight line. The propeller caused the stern to "walk" to starboard, and putting the rudder to port provided little help. Robado had to back and fill with a series of reverse and forward thrusts while working the wheel like a madman. It was as if a troop of chimpanzees had invaded the pilot house and gotten intrigued with the signal pedestal and steering wheel. The chief was working even more frantically below, because this old engine had to be shut off and started again for each direction change—there was no neutral gear and no clutch, and the crankshaft had to be cranked by hand one way or the other to start it in either of the directions. It was like starting a semi tractor with a Model T crank handle every thirty seconds, clockwise for reverse, counterclockwise for forward. The engine command telegraph was ringing so often it sounded like a fire drill.

As the immediate danger of a collision with the bridge seemed to have abated, some of the young student techs wandered back out on the foredeck. They noticed a lot of people leaning out of office windows alongside the river watching the debacle. Some of the guys on the deck waved at the attractive secretaries that were among the rubberneckers. When the young women waved back, the guys started hollering up to the girls, attempting to hook up with them.

"Go tell Tyson to shut those damn kids up," the Captain growled to the first mate. "This is no fucking picnic." The mate ran down the stairway.

"Cut it out you guys," Paul shouted to the students, who waved once more but got quiet. Paul then turned to the mate. "Apologize to Cap for me, okay?"

"I will," replied the mate, who was staring over at the riverbank on the starboard side. "Hey, it looks like there is just enough dock space right there. That's an excursion boat dock, but the boat must be out on its waterfront cruise right now. Get some people ready with the hawsers and heaving lines, and I'll tell Cap about it. He's been busy just getting control and probably hasn't seen that dock yet."

Paul got a couple of student techs and a deckhand busy feeding the hawsers through the hawseholes up over the railings and tying heaving lines to them. Paul stood by with the heaving line for the bow line and watched the pilot house for orders. Captain Robado was able to eventually jockey the *Halcyon* close enough to the dock and called out the order to throw the heaving lines to a couple of dockhands who were watching the whole thing, finally ending the ten minutes of pandemonium. But Robado still had to hope that the State Street bridge would get fixed soon so that he could relinquish the excursion boat's dock space. The people in the cars backed up on State Street obviously were impatient too.

The cacophanous honking bounced all around the glass and concrete building faces.

Soon the chief appeared at the door to the bridge. "Christ Cap, what was going on? I thought somebody shot you with a Taser up here or something."

"I rather it had been that," replied Robado. He took the chief out on the port bridge wing and pointed at the State Street bridge. The chief looked at it, turned to see how close the Wabash bridge was behind them, and took note of the strong wind. He nodded.

"When will they ever retire this old tub and give us a twin screw boat?" asked the chief. "Or maybe some bow and stern thrusters."

"Exactly. This was like maneuvering a galleon full of drunken one-armed oarsmen in a typhoon. But you did great down there, Chief. Saved my job."

They went down to dinner in the wardroom.

An hour later a radio call came in that the State Street bridge was ready, and Robado got the *Halcyon* underway. Their destination was just the other side of the bridge, and they were tied up again in fifteen minutes. The crew headed for the bars, but Paul stayed aboard and made a call to his dad. Brian Tyson was a wealthy businessman who lived in a lakefront home in Evanston. They made a plan to get together while the radar was being serviced on Saturday.

Chapter 17

While Paul had been directing the work at the final sampling station near Chicago, Joan was finishing up her activities at the fish hatchery. She had participated in measuring the growth statistics of the current crops of juvenile salmon and trout that were being reared for stocking lakes in the new season. Though she helped with all of the species of both types of fish, she was interested specifically in the data for the Coho salmon, her research focus. In return, she was allowed to take twelve Coho juveniles for her research. She filled her plastic bucket with hatchery water, netted the fish and placed them in the bucket. Placing the lid on the bucket, she thanked the hatchery director and brought the bucket to her Blazer.

Joan stopped for a leisurely dinner at a roadside restaurant on U.S. 31 halfway back to Traverse City. An equally leisurely drive the rest of the way back was very pleasant with the early evening sun glowing on the roadside poplars, meadows, and cherry orchards. Arriving at the institute at 7 p.m., she brought the bucket of Coho into the lab. No one was there, and she turned the lights on.

Joan set the bucket on the floor near her fish tanks and approached her desk. The white plastic tub from Baines Biological stopped her in her tracks. *What the hell is this?* The tub seemed to have appeared out of nowhere, as surprising as if someone had left a bouquet of roses on her desk. Then she read the label on the top. *Oh, the jellyfish.*

Linda must have ordered them early this term—we don't do Cnidaria for another two weeks. Linda was the intro bio lab coordinator. Joan assumed that Linda had brought them to the lab while Joan was at the hatchery. *Funny she didn't leave a note or anything. Maybe we are supposed to do the Cnidaria sooner this term. Well I'll call her in the morning.* Joan decided to take the top off of the tub so that the animals would not run out of oxygen in the meantime.

Joan brought a net over to the fish bucket and transferred three Cohos into each of her four tanks. She watched them for a while to make sure they were adjusting to the new environment. They all began swimming into the current of the circulating water and looked fine. With a tired yawn she went to the door, shut off the lights to leave, and was startled again by the jellyfish tub on her desk. A pale green light glowed up out of it. She walked over and looked into the tub. The undulating medusas were unmistakably bioluminescent. *Holy crow. I never knew these things were bioluminescent. They're not, damn it. Has Baines developed a new strain to catch the interest of the students or something? What a great marketing ploy. I can't wait to talk to Linda about this.*

Joan turned back toward the door and left the lab. She drove to her apartment, so tired from the day that it was all she could do to undress before tumbling into bed in a deep sleep.

Chapter 18

Later that evening at Whitetail Lake, Kevin Sarginson was walking in the pale moonlight along the lake near the public boat ramp with his friend Ryan, who had arrived with his family at their cottage earlier that day. Kevin had been impatiently waiting for days now to show Ryan the glowing things that were swimming everywhere now, and he was so excited that he kept dropping the minnow net he had brought along to try to catch the things.

"There are some right over there," said Kevin. "Turn off the flashlight."

They sat down at the narrow beach, removed their shoes and socks, and rolled up their pants. They needed to wade out a little way to reach the cluster of jellyfish that glowed tantalizingly just offshore. They started taking careful steps out into the water, trying not to scare the things away. Suddenly they heard a loud car engine and saw headlights coming down the gravel road toward the boat ramp. Afraid it might be drunken teenagers who could make trouble for them, Kevin and Ryan backed out of the water and ran back into a grove of hemlocks. They stopped to watch the car pull up and park near the boat dock. The boy and the girl who got out of the car looked like high school kids, and they indeed looked like they were a little tipsy on something. An empty beer can fell out of the car just before the girl closed the door on her side of the car.

"Look over here," the boy said. "Here's some of those glowing things I told you about. I saw them last night when my brother and I were messing around out here."

"Drinking around out here, you mean," replied the girl.

"Yeah, well duh. Hey babe, let's go skinny dipping. It will be like when my parents and I swam in the bioluminescent water in Puerto Rico last winter. It's great. You make a glowing wake as you swim."

"I don't know Bret. It seems creepy to me, and it's too chilly."

"Oh come on. Have another beer and let's get naked."

"Oookaaay…"

Kevin and Ryan couldn't believe what they were about to see. They'd seen plenty of pictures of naked women, but to be within twenty yards of a real one was beyond their wildest dreams.

The boy opened the car door and pulled out two cans of beer and cracked the pop-tops. He and the girl leaned against the hood and sucked them down in a few long swallows. They kicked off their flip-flops, pulled off their tee shirts and dropped their shorts onto the gravel. Underwear followed quickly, and the boy took the girl by the hand to the edge of the lake.

"I don't know…" said the girl.

"Come on. There's a bunch of them right out there. Dive in with me."

They ran several steps out into the water and dove in. They swam a couple of strokes and dove down into the cluster of jellyfish.

Kevin and Ryan watched in horror as the two swimmers burst up to the surface screaming. They swam back toward shore and staggered to the edge of the beach with glowing globs stuck all over their bodies. They made a few futile attempts to brush them off and then collapsed on the sand. They writhed and moaned for a few moments and then went silent and still.

Kevin and Ryan ran to the stricken swimmers, but didn't know what to do. Kevin was afraid to tell his parents what he was out here seeing, but these people needed help. The boys ran to Kevin's house. "Dad. Two people are hurt over by the boat ramp. You gotta do something!"

Kevin's dad grabbed his cell phone and followed Kevin and Ryan back to the boat ramp.

"Don't touch them dad," cried Kevin. "Maybe those things are what killed Buck."

Kevin's dad drew back his hand from the boy he was about to examine on the sand. "I don't think they are breathing," he said. He pulled out his cell phone and dialed 911.

CHAPTER 19

Saturday morning Joan tried to ignore her alarm clock, but that was hopeless. Besides, she needed to get back to the lab to check on her fish. She quickly dressed in khaki shorts and a blue RULI tee shirt, and choked down some bagels with peanut butter and jam. She got a coffee-to-go at the shop next to her building and went to her Blazer for the drive to the institute.

In her lab, Joan looked at her new Coho juveniles in their tanks for a while, and was satisfied that they were still doing well. She checked on the water temperature and the circulation controls; they were all okay. She then turned her attention to the tub of jellyfish that still puzzled her. She called the bio lab coordinator to find out what was going on, but got Linda's voicemail.

"Hey Linda, it's Joan. What's up with the jellyfish carton? Isn't it early for them? And why are they glowing in the dark now? Give me a call."

Joan looked more closely into the tub, and noticed that a couple of the animals were floating on the surface, apparently dying or dead. She reached her hand toward them to pull them out, but stopped. She knew they were harmless—she'd handled them several times before in class—but was concerned about bacterial contamination from the dead animals that she might accidently transfer to her fish.

She pulled on some vinyl gloves and scooped the two jellyfish out. Halfway over to the waste basket the animals slid out of her hand and landed on her bare thigh, where they stuck as the tentacles shot out their tethered barbs into her skin. She bent to pick them off and froze in sudden intense pain. She screamed, staggered a couple of steps and collapsed on the floor.

The first of the cascade of toxins was wrecking the membranes of her blood cells, which were swelling and bursting, rapidly reducing oxygen transport. That first toxin then triggered the action of the other toxins that began eating away at heart and nerve tissue function; Joan's heart raced arhythmically, and her blood pressure skyrocketed. Her lung and brain tissues began swelling with fluid. Gasping for breath, Joan began hearing the sound of a rushing waterfall and seeing white dancing spots of light.

Joan's cell phone began ringing just as everything went blank.

On the *Halcyon* in Chicago, Paul had his cell phone to his ear and he was hearing a voicemail answer. "Hi, this is Joan Brockton. Leave a message and I'll get back to you."

Surprised that Joan did not pick up, Paul left a message. "Hey Joanie. Give me a call."

CHAPTER 20

After leaving his voice message to Joan, Paul got up and filled his coffee mug in the galley and returned to the wardroom, where a few people including Carol Martin were lingering over a late breakfast. Captain Robado was on the bridge with electronic technicians from the marina who were working on the ship's radar. Paul called his dad to confirm their plans to get together, and then got into a conversation with Martin about her background and her research.

"I went to Illinois Urbana-Champaign for my undergrad and my Ph.D. at Wisconsin before my postdoc at Minnesota."

"Big Ten all the way, right?" said Paul.

"Yeah. I get confused as hell come football season. But it's the Fighting Illini in the end. Even though they tragically had to eliminate Chief Illiniwek, the best part of halftime."

"Well, I have to admit that he was pretty cool, even though I was at Northwestern, and my roommate Craig Basham was a starting linebacker there. Have you met Craig yet, by the way?"

"No I haven't, but I've heard about him. Chief environmental watchdog in northern Michigan, right?"

"Watchdog and executioner," replied Paul as he answered his ringing cell phone.

"Paul, this is Craig."

"My god Craig, how do you do that? We are talking about you right now, for crying out loud. Ran out of useful topics."

"Paul, I've got some bad news."

Paul had a flash of panic. *Joan? Car crash? No way.* "Last time you said that to me on the phone they were charging me with murder one." Paul was talking about when Ron Withers finally died of his injury two years ago.

"Well, unfortunately death is involved here too." Paul's blood pressure shot back up. "Whitetail Lake has struck again," Basham continued. "But this time it's not otters and dogs. Two high school kids were killed last night. They were skinny dipping, and came out of the water covered with jellyfish. They were dead when EMS got to them. They think it's the jellyfish. One of the paramedics touched one without gloves and got real sick."

Paul recovered momentarily from fear regarding Joan, but was still stunned by this news.

"Christ Craig, those things are harmless. What's going on?"

"Evidently they're not harmless anymore. And they're saying these bastards glow in the dark. They've got 'no swimming' signs up all around the lake and they chained off the boat ramp and have a 'no boating' sign there."

"Unbelievable. Glow in the dark? There's some kind of genetic hanky-panky going on here. I need to talk to some people, starting right here with Carol Martin, our new faculty member. By the way, any action on the fertilizer dumping in the river?"

"We've been watching, but nothing so far. We'll keep at it."

"Okay. I'll call you later."

Ending the call, Paul turned to Carol Martin and described the situation to her.

"I've never heard of anything like this. This is amazing. Let me go online and see what I can find. See if there is some rogue strain of freshwater jellyfish that is becoming invasive, maybe transported by waterfowl or something. Whatever, if it really is the jellyfish, they're going to have to start thinking about killing them off in Whitetail Lake before they get spread around to other lakes."

"Oh boy," replied Paul.

Martin went to her computer, and Paul went out on deck to wait for his dad to arrive from Evanston.

Paul showed his dad around the ship, and they went to a nearby coffee shop to chat. Paul filled him in on the tragic events going on in Traverse City.

"My god, that's incredible. Kids dying?"

"Yep."

They chatted some more, until 10:30 a.m. when Paul's cell phone rang again. He looked at the caller ID assuming Joan was finally returning his call. But it was a Roland University call.

"Hello?"

"Paul?"

"Yep."

"This is Dave Washington." It was the marine superintendant at the institute. "I've got some really bad news."

"Oh, I've already heard about the deaths out at Whitetail Lake."

Washington paused a beat. "This is not about that, not exactly. Paul, Joan is in critical condition at the hospital. She got hit with the same animals that those kids were."

Paul's vision narrowed down to a small tunnel of light. He tried to swallow but couldn't. He tried to think of what to say.

"She was out at the lake?" Paul finally asked.

"No. This was right in her lab. There was a plastic tub of those animals on her desk, and two of them were on her leg when they found her on the floor. A student assistant came in and found her that way."

Paul still had trouble talking. "How and why in hell did that get on her desk? And how bad is she? Those kids are dead."

"I'm afraid that she is comatose and extremely critical. Kidneys are beginning to show signs of shutting down. As for how and why the tub of animals is there, this is another whole aspect of the bad news. The cops came in here to search the lab, and found one of her lab notebooks on her desk that has a whole protocol for creating transgenic freshwater jellies with box jelly toxin genes. And plans to spike a lake with them. And further plans to spike the bay with them. They're putting 'no swimming' signs up on the beaches of West Bay. They have a warrant for Joan's arrest when and if she recovers. Paul, I'm terribly sorry to tell you about this disaster."

Paul could hear his pulse pounding in his skull like a bass drum. He reached for a glass of water and knocked it over onto the floor where it splashed and shattered all over the place. His dad stared with his jaw ajar as he watched Paul take punch after punch of the obviously catastrophic news coming through the phone.

"This is just totally impossible," Paul managed to say. "Dave, I have got to get back there somehow." Paul started thinking rationally now that he had to come up with a specific plan of action. "Listen, Carol Martin can take over here. She has caught onto the routine extremely quickly, and she directed several of the stations yesterday. Let me go ask her if she will do that. Will you see if you can clear that with Director Tollefson, so I can go catch a plane?"

"Sounds fine to me, Paul. Tollefson is here, and I'll talk to her right away. Call me after you talk to Carol."

"Dave, do Joan's parents know?"

"They're on the way up from Farmington."

"Okay. I'll call back soon."

Paul ended the call and filled his dad in with the sordid details.

"I'll go get my car and drive you to Midway Airport." Brian Tyson left the coffee shop to get his car from the nearby parking structure.

Paul returned to the *Halcyon* to find Carol. She was in her small stateroom on the main deck, still working the computer. She went pale as Paul told her all of the news.

"Paul, I'm so sorry about Joan. If she had only a couple of those jellies on her, maybe she got a small enough hit that she will survive it. The two kids were covered with them, right?"

"That's what Craig said."

"Now, if those things have box jelly toxin genes, it is imperative to somehow get them all killed off at that lake, including larval and polyp stages. Let me think about that. Meanwhile, yes of course I will take over the cruise if Dr. Tollefson okays it."

Paul called David Washington, and learned that he had permission to fly back to Traverse. Paul said he would call from the airport when he knew when he would arrive up there. Washington said he would pick him up at the airport. Paul called for flight information and learned that he would have to connect through Detroit, a seven hour trip for nearly a thousand bucks. He decided to rent a car and get there sooner for a fraction of the cost, and he called Dave Washington back to tell him this. He went up to the bridge to fill the captain in on the plan, and entered his stateroom to pack. Paul's dad drove Paul to a car rental office, and Paul was on his way.

Chapter 21

It took Paul an hour and a half to get out of the city and onto the Skyway into Indiana, and then traffic thinned out. No longer preoccupied with the traffic, Paul dwelled fully on the horror of the situation that awaited him in Traverse City. The thought of Joan's possibly imminent death brought waves of panic attacks that had him hyperventilating and getting hand cramps on the steering wheel. *Can I have a heart attack at my age?* He tried to force himself to think about Whitetail Lake and what to do there. Finally he had to break his safe driving rule and call Craig Basham on his cell phone.

"Craig, have you heard about Joan?"

"Yes, I heard it on the news. I'm at the hospital now. They won't tell me anything. God I'm sorry Paul."

"Do you know the cops have a warrant for her arrest?"

"Yes, the news people are saying there is evidence that she is involved in the Whitetail Lake deaths, which is bullshit of course."

"Craig, you will need to get Hal Holmes in on this." Holmes was the criminal defense lawyer that helped Basham defend Paul two years ago in his murder case.

"Already called him. He's in."

"How in hell did that goddamn bucket of jellyfish get on her desk? And how did whoever did it come up with this transgenic nightmare?"

"No idea, but unfortunately it is well known that Joan is a pretty good gene jockey, which doesn't help. Listen, I have a feeling that you are going to be questioned about this."

"No doubt. And I have some questions for them. Craig we need to talk about Whitetail Lake too. Carol Martin pointed out that the jellyfish population is going to have to be destroyed there somehow. You need to call the Michigan Department of Environmental Quality to make sure they are thinking about that. And meanwhile something has to be done to prevent the transfer of the juvenile stages from being transferred to other lakes by way of wildlife, especially waterfowl."

"The MDEQ is already onto the waterfowl thing. They have people out there shooting shotguns at everything that flies into the lake's airspace. The whole area is excited about a special unlimited duck and goose season that has been opened there. They can't collect anything that falls in the lake, but anything that hits the ground is fair game, so to speak. On the TV video clips it sounds like a firefight in Afganistan out there. By the way, they say the jellyfish glow in the dark."

"Really? Probably a marker gene to keep tabs on the gene transfer. Well that can be useful. Monitor nearby lakes and the bay at night so that if they do appear anywhere else we'll know before someone gets hurt again."

"I'll pass that on to the MDEQ."

"Craig, I'm getting suspicious that the dumping of fertilizer in the river is somehow connected to all this, now that we know that there is a threat of putting the jellies in the bay. Maybe the plankton bloom in the bay is supposed to jack up the food-base for them."

"Didn't think of that. Holy shit. I'll try to increase the surveillance at Eighth Street."

"Okay. Well, I'll be there in about three hours, and will come to the hospital directly."

"Okay Paul. See you then."

In Jerry Fenner's trailer another phone conversation was going on.

"You didn't tell me people were going to die."

"Like what?"

"Two high school kids were killed last night by those damn things."

"Perfect."

"Brockton's critical."

"Even better."

"Christ Griffin. You got me involved in murder here. I'm shittin' bricks up here and you're down there sunbathing and banging native twat."

"Calm down dude. They'll never pin this on you. A construction worker making a transgenic jellyfish? Just finish out the program. A few more bags of fertilizer in the river, and I'll send you one more tub for the bay. Then you get your last two grand and lay low. No problem."

"They got 'no swimming' signs up all over the damn place. They're shootin' ducks off the lake so they don't spread the slimy fuckers to other lakes."

"Good. General panic. But there'll be assholes who will ignore the signs."

"Good god. Look, I'll think about it."

But Fenner didn't actually have to think very long. He didn't tell Griffin, but he had gotten laid off from his construction job yesterday, and couldn't walk away from the additional two thousand dollars.

CHAPTER 22

At 4:30 p.m. Paul pulled into the parking lot of the hospital, which was bathed in the afternoon sunlight. His heart was hammering at his rib cage as he walked into the emergency lobby, where he found Joan's parents talking quietly with Craig Basham. He silently embraced Joan's mom and then her dad. Nobody knew what to say, and they just nodded at each other with moist eyes. Craig shook Paul's hand and squeezed his shoulder for a moment. Joan's dad finally spoke.

"There's no change. Deep coma, heart weak, kidneys not good. They said we could bring you in to see her."

Paul nodded, still speechless. He followed the parents into the ICU; he was totally unprepared for what he saw. Joan was ghostly pale and still, IV in her left arm, eyes taped shut, a catheter bag hanging from the bed rail less than a quarter full of dark urine, a ventilator sighing in rhythm with the barely perceptible rising and falling of her chest. The cacophonous heart monitor sounded like the beeping of reverse warning signals from two or three construction vehicles backing and filling at a jobsite.

"I love you Joanie," whispered Paul close to her ear. "I know you're in there. You'll be back. Take your time, we'll be here." He wanted to think he saw a change of expression on her face, but there was no such thing. He held her hand for a moment, and then nodded to Joan's mom.

"Thanks Mrs. Brockton."

"Thank you, Paul."

They quietly left the room and returned to the lobby.

"You must be exhausted from your trip," said Joan's dad. "Things are stable here for now, so why don't you get some rest at home and come back in the morning. We can keep in touch by phone. Craig is kindly letting us stay in his guest room, so we will be close by the hospital."

"I guess I'd better do that. Thanks Mr. Brockton, and thanks Craig, for helping out."

"You got it," replied Craig.

Paul drove to the Budget car lot, turned in the rental, and got a ride to the institute where his Mustang was parked. He decided to stop in the lab before heading home. He put his sea bag in his car and walked into the limnology building, and as he walked down the hall toward the Perry lab he saw two men in dark suits sitting on folding chairs. *Here we go.* They stood up as he approached them.

"Mr. Tyson?"

"None other."

"I'm detective lieutenant Parker, and this is detective sergeant Baldwin."

Paul looked them over. Both cops wore mustaches and had bad hair dyes. Parker was trim and his suit fit well. Baldwin would never be able to button his suit coat around a belly that hung over his belt like a sack of hog feed.

Parker continued, "We're from the county sheriff's office. Can we talk for a few minutes?"

"Come on in."

The detectives brought the chairs into the lab and invited Paul to sit in the one at his desk. Dr. Perry came out of his office and told Paul he was sorry about this intrusion. Detective Parker thanked Perry for talking with them and asked him to leave, which he did.

"Okay Mr. Tyson, we need to know what you know about Joan Brockton and what your involvement with her has been in recent weeks."

"She is a first rate scientist, an exceptional human being, and she and I are very close."

"Close enough to work with her on a transgenic project?"

"I don't know genes from jockstraps. Joan does for sure, but she has never done transgenic work. Never trained for it."

"How do you know that?"

"I've known her for three years, and I know her background."

"I'll bet you know her *back round* real well," snickered Detective Baldwin. "Get it, *around back*?" Baldwin laughed until his smoker's cough kicked in. Paul stared at Baldwin while he rattled and bounced for several seconds, and then replied.

"You can take that comment and blow it up your own ass and go jerk-off someplace, if you can even reach it, you fat fuck."

Baldwin heaved himself up off his chair with balled fists and a red face. Detective Parker grabbed Baldwin's arm and eased him back onto the chair.

"Let's slow down a little here, Bruce."

"Oh, now we're playing good-cop-bad-cop, are we?" said Paul.

"The prosecutor did say you are a testy one," Baldwin said, breathing hard.

"That asshole was wrong about me two years ago, and he's wrong about Joan now. So you guys can just go screw doughnuts." Paul's anger was reaching full fury now, a rage he hadn't felt for two years since the days of Ron Wither's plagiarism and Paul's indictment for murder.

"Look," said Parker. "We've got two kids lying in the morgue, and a tub of the same critters that killed them sitting on Brockton's desk along with a data book in her handwriting describing the gene work that produced them and plans for putting them in lakes. Help us out here."

"Look yourself. I just got here from seeing Joan in the ICU. She is this far from being dead herself." Paul held his thumb and finger a half-centimeter apart. "If she did what you are claiming she did, she is way too smart to let those damn things come in contact with herself. She obviously had no idea how dangerous they were. So who planted them in her lab?"

"What about the notebook?" replied Parker.

"Can I see the notebook? See if it's really her handwriting?"

"No you can't. We have handwriting experts for that."

"Does it have her fingerprints on it?"

"Can't tell you that. But we have something better. Some strands of her hair seem to be in it. We're checking the DNA against hair that's on her hairbrush in her drawer."

Paul swallowed and looked at the floor. "Well," replied Paul, "I don't know who would have planted that stuff in her lab, but some son of a bitch did, and I will find out who, whether or not you bother to try. By the way, what prompted you guys to come and look in her lab in the first place?"

"A little birdie told us."

"Oh come on."

"We got an anonymous note in the mail."

"Planted by whoever is setting her up."

"What kind of enemies does she have that would do that?" asked Parker.

"What kind of enemies does she have that would give *her* a motive to pull this awful stunt?" Paul retorted.

The detectives stood up, and Detective Parker handed Paul one of his business cards. He told Paul they would probably be talking to him again soon, and left.

After Paul sat a few minutes to simmer down a little, he got up and got the Wisconsin plankton net from a cabinet and took it outside and onto the dock. He walked out to the end and looked down at the water. He saw no jellyfish, but the plankton bloom was too thick to see much below the surface, as he expected. He tossed and retrieved the net several times, and it came back jam packed. There were no jellies in the net.

He brought the net back into the lab, poured some of the sample into a class beaker, and took that into a windowless equipment room and shut the door with the lights off. He was looking for any bioluminescent plankton, which would be the larval stage of the jellyfish. No pinpoints of light swimming around. Back in the main lab room, he placed a drop of the plankton concentrate on a slide and examined it under a microscope. He couldn't find anything that looked like a jellyfish planula. So far so good, but that didn't mean there weren't some out there somewhere.

Paul rinsed the net in the sink, hung it to dry, and closed up the lab for the trip to his boat in Elk Rapids.

Chapter 23

Driving toward Elk Rapids on U.S. 31 north of Acme, Paul was thinking hard about the last question that Detective Parker asked him. *Who in hell would pull that vicious transgenic stunt and try to pin it on Joan? There is no way in anybody's hell that she would do such a thing.* Paul felt as angry and depressed as he had been two years ago while driving on this same stretch of 31 after he had seen Joan getting into Larry Griffin's car in the institute lot, a few days after Paul and Joan had had their falling out. The image came to him now.

Griffin! The scumbag tried to seduce her and she kicked him out. She helped get him thrown out of RULI when he molested those students of his. Could he be that demonic that he would do this just to retaliate? Get people killed, for Christ sake? How did he do it? Where the hell is he?

The thoughts swirled around in Paul's head like a load of socks in a washing machine. It was hard to believe that Griffin would do this, but who else?

Paul's thoughts were interrupted by a phone call; the caller ID on his cell phone indicated it was Carol Martin. This time Paul pulled to the side of the road to take the call.

"Hi Paul, sorry to intrude. How is Joan?"

"Not good. Touch and go. We may lose her."

"Is she stable at least?"

"Not totally. Kidneys have stripped some gears."

"I'm still going to predict that she will pull through. Think that way, Paul."

"Thanks, Carol. What's up in Chicago?"

"They got the radar fixed, and we're heading north tomorrow. As you know, a set of stations straight up the lake, and we will be getting in late tomorrow night."

"Good. Thanks again for pinch hitting for me."

"No problem," replied Carol. "See you soon."

Paul ended the call and dialed the cell phone number that was on Detective Parker's business card.

"Parker."

"Detective, this is Paul Tyson. I thought of someone who might be mad enough at Joan to make big trouble for her."

"Oh, and who would that be?"

"His name is Larry Griffin." Paul ran though the history of Joan's traumatic encounter with Griffin and Griffin's ultimate fate.

"So where is he now?"

"Don't know."

"How can we find out?"

"Don't know."

"This is a big help."

"I guess I'm on my own here. Just write his name down, will you? Run his name in your data base or whatever you guys do."

"Okay, but don't you get too fancy out there, Tyson."

"It's a free country, Parker."

Paul drove the rest of the way to Elk Rapids, stopped for a sandwich and salad to go, and went to his boat. Down in the salon he was glad to find that he had plenty of beer in his fridge. He cracked one open now and took it up to the cockpit with his bag of food.

The harbor was peaceful, with a number of boaters enjoying the developing sunset in their cockpits. The usual sound of bleating seagulls was music to Paul's ears despite his state of mind. He tried to feel some of Carol Martin's optimism about Joan, without much success. Joan should be here in the cockpit where she belonged. It would be a long time, if ever, before that happened.

Paul finished his meal and his beer and went below. He booted up his computer and started searching for Larry Griffin. Google produced nothing more that the publications Griffin had co-authored with Dr. Bates. Paul checked Facebook and the other social media sites. Griffin was on none of them. *Smart guy.* Paul gave up and closed his computer. He went up to the marina building, showered, and returned to *Tondeleyo*. He drank another beer in the cockpit, went below to bed with a paperback novel, and then tried to go to sleep.

Sleep never came that night.

CHAPTER 24

After tossing and turning half the night, walking the docks in the moonlight for an hour and then tossing and turning again for the rest of the night, Paul rose on Sunday morning, ate a quick breakfast and drove to Traverse City. He went straight to the hospital, hoping that Joan's parents would be there this early. They were.

"She had a terrible night," said Mrs. Brockton in the lobby.

"Oh lord. Tell me about it," said Paul.

"She went from dangerously high blood pressure to dangerously low, and her blood cell count became critically low. They were able to successfully provide transfusion support, and are able to stabilize her blood pressure medically. They're still fighting her pulmonary edema with oxygen, dopamine and adrenalin. At least her kidneys did not deteriorate any further. But mostly we have to wait it out."

"There's no antidote treatment?"

"The doctors said that there is a new antidote for the box jelly toxin that effectively counteracts the first toxin in the cascade, but the closest source for it is thousands of miles away, and even if we had it here, it was hours before we knew of the box jelly involvement, way too late for the antidote to have worked. They are ordering some in case there are any more exposures here. They applied acetic acid to the skin of her thigh to immobilize any remaining stinger cells, but it was probably too late for that too."

"So except for basic life support, she's on her own," said Paul. "Obviously the toxins have to wear off—get detoxified by the liver and cleared by the kidneys, I suppose—and then her body has to repair itself."

"Yes," replied Mrs. Brockton. "But it's early yet. They say it's usually about a three-day acute crisis period, and we don't know how much permanent damage has already been done."

Paul's heart sank once again. "Well she's a tough lady. Can I see her?"

"Come on back," said Mrs. Brockton.

Joan was still ghostly pale, not much different from the white sheet that covered her, and was still motionless except for the work of the ventilator that was breathing for her. Her heart monitor beeped a little more steadily, but not much. Paul held her hand again and spoke to her. He knew that some comatose patients can hear people talking to them.

"Come on Joanie, keep fighting. We'll be here every day."

They went back to the lobby, where Joan's lab assistant had arrived and was talking with Craig Basham, also newly arrived.

"Hi Amanda," said Paul "How are you?"

"Fine, but how is Joan?"

"Hanging in there. Tell me about what happened yesterday morning."

"I came into the lab and found Joan unconscious on the floor. I called 911 and went to her. I saw the jellyfish on her right thigh, and thought that might be her problem. I saw that she had gloves on, so I put some on and pulled off the jellyfish. Then I gave her CPR until the paramedics came in. It was awful."

"You saved her life, Amanda."

"I hope it helped. I'm just terribly worried about her."

"We all are. But thanks for what you did."

"I'll help however I can. I'll be working with her doctoral advisor Dr. Pendleton to keep her fish stocks going as best we can till we get her back."

"She'll appreciate that," said Paul.

Paul turned to Craig. "Craig, how about we go out to Whitetail Lake to see what's happening there. I'll fill you in on Joan's status on the way."

Craig agreed. Paul introduced Amanda to the Brocktons, who greeted her warmly and began chatting with her as Paul and Craig left the hospital and walked to Craig's truck.

Chapter 25

On the way out to Whitetail Lake, Paul described Joan's condition to Craig, who nodded darkly as he listened.

"I still can't believe it," said Craig. "And we're so powerless to help."

"Yep."

They could hear the gunfire as they turned onto the gravel road leading to the Whitetail Lake boat ramp. Pickup trucks lined both shoulders; there were dogs in a few of the truck cabs and cages in some of the truck beds with retrievers panting impatiently in them.

"Looks like some of these guys didn't catch the fact that dogs in the water here is a no-no and had to put 'em back in their cages," said Craig. "And the dogs aren't happy about it."

Windblown bird shot hailed down on Basham's hood and roof as he pulled up behind a MDEQ truck in the parking lot. The district chief was sitting in the passenger seat with the door open, shaking his head. "We've got a circular firing squad here," he said to Craig. "I hope we don't kill more people that the jellyfish have."

Every time a duck flew anywhere near the lake a roar of shotgun fire erupted around the lake as though Commodore Perry was re-fighting the Battle of Lake Erie.

"It does seem to be keeping the waterfowl off the lake," the chief said. "I feel sorry for the homeowners out here;

vacations gone to hell. A lot of them have headed back south."

Craig introduced Paul to the chief, and they shook hands.

"What's the plan to get rid of the jellyfish?"

"We're going to go with rotenone," said the chief. "As I'm sure you know, it's the standard treatment we use to make rapid fish kills to census fish communities or eliminate an unwanted invasive population. It breaks down rapidly in the water and is not a long-term problem for the environment; we can restock quickly. However the concentration we use for fish will not be sufficient to get the jellies, especially the larvae. The fish are the most sensitive to rotenone, and invertebrates and even fish eggs tolerate our usual treatments pretty well. We will have to put in maybe ten times the usual amount. That will be done tomorrow. Come on out and watch the fun."

"Okay thanks," said Paul. "Listen, have you got anyone checking for the jellyfish in the bay?"

"Yes we do. But the visibility in the plankton bloom is terrible."

"I know," Paul replied. "Be sure to check at night; they're luminescent. I'm going to be checking the plankton for the larval stage, the planulas. I'm sure Dr. Martin will help when she gets back from the cruise she's on."

"Good. Thanks."

Craig said, "I think right now we'll back on out of here and leave the war zone to you, general."

The chief smirked and nodded.

Heading back northward on Garfield, Sunday traffic was light. A strong wind was rustling the early summer wild flowers in the sunny meadows, and the hemlocks were waving their branches around like a stadium full of rock concert fans.

"Craig, a rather obvious thought finally came to me out of the fog in this thick skull of mine."

"What?"

"Who is the only person on the planet that would pull this stunt and try to get Joan blamed for it in addition to being critically hurt?"

Craig thought a minute. "Oh my god. Griffin. Really?"

"There's just no one else. And I suspect that he knows we can figure it out, the arrogant bastard. But he's likely got himself well hidden somewhere hard to find."

"Where could that be that would give him the opportunity to do the transgenic work? I assume you can't do that in a garage somewhere."

"We heard that he was in med school somewhere. Maybe out of the country. Probably, come to think of it."

"Dozens, maybe hundreds of those. Piece of cake, right Sherlock?"

"Yeah, sure. Hey, here's Eighth Street. Let's go look at the fertilizer dumping venue. I hope we're right that it's somehow connected to Griffin. If we can catch someone at it, maybe we can get to him."

Craig turned left and drove the ten blocks west to the Boardman River and pulled into the parking lot at Boardman Avenue. They got out and walked to the seawall along the river. No more discarded bags, though Paul figured the guy might only make that mistake once.

"How do your people do the surveillance?" asked Paul. "It's kind of open around here."

"We park over in front of that building there, and hide in the shrubbery on this side of it. We get a pretty clear view along the river edge. Your guy Brad is doing a lot of the night shifts. He's really geeked to get this guy."

"Well, if this is connected to Griffin's gig, I very much doubt if it's Griffin himself. He's too smart for that. He's got somebody working for him. Hopefully whoever it is is not so smart and makes a mistake. Maybe I'll take some nights myself now that I'm back."

"Suits me."

They drove back to the hospital and checked in on the Brocktons. Things were the same there. Paul got in his Mustang and drove to the lab, picking up a MickeyD burger for lunch on the way.

The wind had the bay kicked up into a froth, and Paul decided it was too rough to take a boat out for plankton sampling. He got a net sample from off the dock and looked at it in the lab the way he had the day before. No larvae that he could find. He decided to go next door to Joan's lab to look around and maybe talk to her mentor, if he happened to be there. When he got there he found yellow crime-scene tape plastered across the door. He went back to his lab and tried to focus on his own research for a while. He ended up just fiddling with equipment and putting away glassware.

At 5:30 Paul drove back to the hospital. The Brocktons were still there in the lobby. No change in Joan; no better, no worse. Paul suggested that they go to dinner somewhere close by with him. They agreed, and Paul drove them to the brew pub that was his and Joan's favorite. Paul had met them a few times but did not know them well. They were attractive professional people in their late fifties. Joan had obviously gotten her brown eyes and honey blond hair from her mother. Joan's strong chin and straight narrow nose were her father's.

Some draft beers were a welcome temporary respite from the grinding hospital vigil, and the burgers were satisfying. But there was little to talk about at this point, and soon Paul drove them back to the hospital. They all looked in on Joan for a while, and then Paul left and went back to the lab. He decided to wait for the *Halcyon* to get in later in the evening, and help unload samples and equipment. Marine Superintendant Dave Washington was in the institute office, and Paul learned that their ETA was 9:30 p.m. Paul went back to the lab for more mindless fiddling around.

At 9:20 Dave Washington came to Paul's lab door and said, "They're in sight out there."

"Thanks, Dave." They both walked out onto the dock, and they took lines from the deckhands as the ship eased to her berth and rumbled in reverse for a few moments.

When the lines were secure on the bollards, Paul stepped aboard and found Carol Martin. He told her about Joan's status, and about the MDEQ's plan to take her advice and poison the jellies at Whitetail Lake. He told her about the war zone out there with all the shotguns, and that it was working.

"Will they be at it at night too?" Martin asked.

"I guess they'll have to. But those guys with the trucks will love it. Listen, I want to start monitoring the plankton here in the bay to look for jellyfish planulas. Would you like to help?"

"Of course. Let's get started tomorrow. Great project for the rotating student in my lab."

Paul helped get samples and equipment moved into the limnology building for the next hour, and then drove back to Elk Rapids. He was so exhausted after last night's lack of sleep that he fell onto his bunk on *Tondeleyo* in his clothes and was out instantly.

CHAPTER 26

Monday morning Paul got a call from Craig Basham just as he was getting in his car to drive to Traverse City.

"Paul, I know you don't read the papers, but pick one up this morning."

"Why?"

"Just do it."

Paul stopped at the corner drugstore on River Street on his way out of Elk Rapids. He stared at the paper. The huge banner headline blared with the words, NO SWIMMING. The lead article described the whole transgenic jellyfish saga, repeated the coverage of the deaths of the teenagers at Whitetail Lake, and stated that Joan Brockton at the Roland University Limnology Institute was under suspicion of being responsible, even though she herself was in critical condition from contact with the jellyfish. The article finished by describing the panic that was growing in the public about the possibility that the bay will be infested with the lethal animals, and the concern that tourist revenue was in danger of collapsing. The article was accompanied by a photo of a 'no swimming' sign on the beach on West Bay.

Paul threw the paper in the backseat of his car and drove south on U.S. 31 to Traverse City. When he got to the lab, Dr. Perry was there waiting for him.

"Hi Paul. How did it go with the detectives yesterday?"

"Not particularly well. They never seem to want to stretch beyond their initial impression of who to go after for a crime."

"Let's hope it's different this time. Meanwhile, Director Tollefson wants to talk to you about it. Can we go up to her office right now?"

"Sure," replied Paul.

Dr. Karen Tollefson was the internationally known Swedish limnologist who had been recruited by Rynar University to direct the limnology institute several years before, and the no-nonsense scientist had already catapulted RULI into national prominence. The blond woman looked out over her black-framed reading glasses and waved Paul and Dr. Perry into her second floor office. Linda Carter, the introductory biology lab coordinator, was already seated in the room. Paul nodded to Linda, and he and Perry sat down.

"Paul. It's been only two years since our last catastrophe around here. I'm not ready for this. What in the world is going on?"

"Dr. Tollefson, I don't know what to say. I'm blown out of the water myself. The only thing I know for sure is that the only way that stuff got in Joan's lab and in that lake was by way of someone else, and I have a hunch I know who."

"First of all, how is Joan?"

"Still critical but stable last night; I haven't talked to the Brocktons this morning yet."

"Well, we should go over to the hospital after we talk. Now then: I have an appointment to be interviewed by the local TV people, and I need to know as much as I can learn before that. Linda here has told me that she has not ordered any of those freshwater jellies yet for Bio 101 this term. She checked with Baines Biological where she gets them, and they have no record of anyone else from here ever ordering them. The ones she has ordered in past semesters are all accounted for. So that seems to suggest that Joan has not gotten any of those Baines tubs directly herself. Next, what about transgenic work?"

"Like I told the detectives, although she works with genes and is very good at it, she has not done any transgenic work here, nor has anyone else here." Linda Carter nodded in agreement. "And you can check her undergrad transcript; she has no training for it."

"Okay," replied Tollefson. "Oh, Linda, have you been able to get Joan's teaching duties covered?"

"Yes, several of the other TAs have volunteered to take turns teaching her sections while she is out."

"Good. They're good kids. Paul, what's going on at Whitetail Lake?"

Paul described the MDEQ's activities and their plans for rotenone treatment.

"I hope that works. But the surrounding lakes will still need to be monitored in case the jellyfish have gotten transferred into them. Those poor two kids and their families. God I miss Sweden; much gentler place. Do you think the jellyfish can really grow in the bay if they were or will be put there?"

"I would think that the sand bottom and frequent rough surf action would not be favorable. The medusas are fragile and the polyps need a hard substrate. Those things are primarily pond animals. Also, I think the plankton bloom in the bay might be too thick for them. But I think whoever is doing this thinks it will help them grow. Anyway, Carol Martin and I will be helping the MDEQ monitor the bay."

"The public will probably still be frightened. You should contact the county health department and keep them informed about your monitoring."

"I will," said Paul.

"That brings us back to your hunch about who is doing this."

"Larry Griffin is the only one I know with a motive to cause trouble for Joan and for all of us here."

"Could be," said Tollefson. "Any evidence that he is involved?"

"Not so far, and the cops don't seem interested. We're trying to catch whoever is dumping fertilizer into the river. He may be a link."

"Okay. Thank you Paul; this is helpful. Let's go to the hospital; I need to be back at noon."

Director Tollefson, Dr. Perry, Linda Carter and Paul all drove separately and met at the hospital. The Brocktons were in the lobby looking weary and depressed. Paul introduced them to the university people.

"Joan is one of our finest graduate students," said Dr. Tollefson. "We are devastated by this horrible thing."

"Thank you," replied Mrs. Brockton. "We read this morning's paper. We were shocked to learn that Joan is under suspicion for causing all of this herself. How can that possibly be?"

"Joan is not under suspicion by any of us here, I can tell you that," said Tollefson. "We intend to get to the bottom of it somehow. In the meantime we offer any help you may possibly need to cope with getting Joan better. How is she this morning?"

Mrs. Brockton broke down, and Mr. Brockton answered. "She is still critical but stable. They think at this point there is a good chance for survival, but if so, we still don't know when she will come out of her coma, and how much permanent damage has been done."

Dr. Tollefson took his hands in hers, and then did the same with Mrs. Brockton. "We will pray for her."

"Thank you all for coming," Mrs. Brockton managed to say.

Tollefson, Perry and Carter all left to return to the institute, and Paul went with the Brockton's to see Joan in the ICU. He tried again to speak encouraging words in hopes that she might hear him. It was hard not to feel discouraged himself; he kept it out of his voice as best he could.

Back in the lobby Craig Basham had arrived.

"Craig," said Paul, "I'm going to get some plankton samples from the bay with Carol Martin this morning. How about we go back out to Whitetail Lake this afternoon to watch the rotenone treatment?"

"Yep. Just call me when you're ready."

Craig sat down to chat with the Brocktons, and Paul excused himself to return to the institute.

Chapter 27

Paul drove back to the lab and found Brad Barlow there mixing stock reagents. He invited Brad to go out with him and Dr. Martin on the *Chinook* for some plankton samples. They grabbed the Wisconsin net and a crate of sample bottles and went down the hall to Carol Martin's lab.

"Ready to go fishing for jellies?" said Paul.

"Let's go," Martin replied.

They stopped in the main office to pick up the boat keys and went out to the docks. It was calm and sunny, good sampling conditions. Paul warmed up the engine, Brad cast off, and they motored out into the plankton bloom along the shore of the bay. It was wider and longer than it had been last week.

"How's the surveillance at the river going?" Paul asked Barlow.

"Boring, but he's bound to be there soon. Unless he's done now. Hope not."

"Maybe I'll try it tonight," said Paul.

They started at the west end of the bloom and did net tosses every fifty meters along the bloom until they reached the eastern end of it. They also sampled in the city marina and back in the RULI harbor. They tied up the boat and brought the samples into Carol Martin's lab.

"Carol, if you and Brad could work on these today, that would be great. I want to go out to Whitetail Lake with Craig and observe the rotenone operation."

"Can do. I'll get my rotating student to work on it too. Brad, let's go get some lunch first."

Paul called Craig Basham and then drove to Craig's office to pick him up. They stopped at a Taco Bell, and munched on burritos on the way out to Whitetail Lake.

"The container of jellies on Joan's desk was a product of Baines Biological. Linda Carter, the intro bio coordinator, has learned from Baines that no one here except Linda has ever ordered freshwater jellies from them. And she has never had any disappear from her prep room."

"Well, that's a useful fact for our side. The cops keep sending a man around to make sure Joan isn't going anywhere."

"Figures."

As they approached Whitetail Lake, they found that the shotgun barrages were down to an occasional blast. Two MDEQ boats were out on the lake, and only MDEQ personnel were standing by with guns. Birds were avoiding the area now anyway. The district chief explained what was going on to Paul and Craig as they stood on the boat ramp dock.

One boat was slowly motoring around while a man poured the contents of plastic jugs into the prop wash of the outboard. Because the rotenone applied at the surface would never mix down into the lower layer of water, the cold "hypolimnion," the other boat sat still in various places and lowered a container down near the bottom. The container was an open mouthed canister with a line duct-taped to its bottom end so that it would tip over and empty when pulled back to the surface. They had to hope that the rotenone would eventually mix around down there, although that would be slow, because that water is isolated from the wind turbulence that mixes the warm upper "epilimnion."

The chief continued, "As you probably know, rotenone inhibits basic aerobic cellular respiration, and therefore is toxic to everything that uses oxygen. We are trying to put in enough that we actually kill everything. Therefore, we are going to have one hell of a mess of dead stuff. We will try to collect as much as we can of whatever floats to the surface. That's what the honey wagon over there is for."

Paul and Craig watched for an hour or so, by which time dead fish had begun to float to the surface in large clumps. As hoped for, dead jellyfish appeared among the bass, perch and bluegills. All of the MDEQ personnel were equipped with hazmat suits and breathing masks, and as workers began collecting the carnage with nets and barrels the chief warned them again not to touch any of it with bare skin.

"Quite an operation" said Paul to the district chief.

"Yep. Hope it works. The lake will take quite a while to recover from this. Meanwhile we have to monitor it and the surrounding lakes for the damn things, as well as the bay. What's this about the possible involvement of a grad student at the university? Please tell me that's not true."

"Trust me it's not; she's a victim, not a perp, but the circumstantial information they have is a problem for her until we find the bastard who has done this."

"Whoever did it is a terrorist. Is Homeland Security involved?"

"Not to my knowledge, but that may be next," replied Paul. "Well, we will be in touch. Thanks for your hard work here."

Paul and Craig got in Paul's Mustang and drove back to town. As it was late in the afternoon, they decided to take a break at a brew pub near Craig's office.

CHAPTER 28

As Paul and Craig nursed their second glasses of draft, their attention was drawn to the local news on the large flat-screen TV above the bar. It was showing a video recording of the interview of RULI director Dr. Tollefson by a field reporter in Tollefson's office.

"Director Tollefson," the reporter began, "the mayor and the chamber of commerce president are responding to the public outrage at the recent deaths from some kind of new jellyfish that has been introduced into at least one of our lakes, and they are calling for an investigation into the role of your institute here in this situation."

"We are devastated by the tragic loss of life of the two innocent teenagers at Whitetail Lake," replied Dr. Tollefson. "They could not have known the danger that the normally harmless freshwater jellyfish posed to them. The creation and release of a transgenic strain with lethal toxins was an heinous crime that needs to be solved quickly. Meanwhile, Whitetail Lake is being treated as we speak by the MDEQ to kill them there, and the MDEQ and our own scientists will be monitoring other water bodies in the area to make sure these animals do not appear anywhere else. As for the bay, our scientists actually do not think the jellyfish can grow and survive there, but they are monitoring it closely and cooperating with the environmental health division of the county health department. I recommend that you televise some pictures of these creatures and encourage the public in the area to report any sightings of them. Also emphasize that the poisonous ones glow in the dark."

"What about the rumor that a graduate student at the university is responsible?" asked the reporter.

"That student is in critical condition at the hospital, a victim of the jellyfish herself. She was obviously unaware that they are toxic. Despite some puzzling circumstances, we have no doubt that she had nothing to do with this other than being a victim."

"Do you have any idea who else could have done this?"

"We do have an idea, but I cannot comment beyond that at this time."

"Thank you, Director Tollefson," said the reporter, who turned to the camera and began a wrap-up statement. The barkeep switched the channel to CNN and Paul and Craig turned back to their beers.

"She did a good job," said Craig.

"She is very good at everything she does. We are lucky to have her."

Paul was so tired and stressed from the whole thing that he ordered a third round.

"My wife's not going to be happy with me coming home smelling like I've been to a frat party," said Craig, but he picked up the glass anyway and then noticed a banner headline scrolling across the bottom of the TV screen proclaiming "2 deaths in a Michigan lake." He pointed it out to Paul, and they listened. Two CNN stories later the anchor read the "Breaking News" story from the teleprompter.

"We have learned that over the weekend two high school students died after swimming among some freshwater jellyfish in a small lake near Traverse City, Michigan. While freshwater jellyfish are normally harmless to humans, these animals apparently were a strain that had been genetically altered to contain some of the toxins in the lethal marine box jelly that have killed at least sixty-seven people in Australia in recent years. Under suspicion for creating and releasing these transgenic creatures is a graduate student at Traverse City's Rynar University. University officials deny this allegation on behalf of the student, who is currently in critical condition from exposure to the animals herself. We will bring you more details when they become available." The anchor moved on to the next story.

"Oh boy," said Paul

"Just what we need," said Craig.

Down in Isla Colombo, Larry Griffin had been watching CNN in his apartment on the med school campus. As the story unfolded he whooped and pumped his fist in the air. "YES. YES." He drained the last of his rum bottle and opened another one.

Over in the infirmary Juanita decided she had waited long enough to go home that she probably would not encounter Griffin on the way to her car, and left to go home. When she got home she cooked and ate a simple meal and then sat down and booted up her computer to resume her web search for job opportunities. The home page that came up was a news site. Quickly scanning the headlines, she noticed one of them that said "Jellyfish kill teenagers in Michigan, U.S.A." Curious, she clicked on the story. It was essentially the same report that CNN was running.

Juanita stiffened at the keyboard, her thoughts racing. *Transgenic freshwater jellyfish with box jelly genes. Can this be a coincidence? Larry once told me that he was in grad school in northern Michigan and hated it there. Hated the people there. Madre de Dios. What has he done?*

Juanita did not know what to do about what she suspected—no, what she was sure of. She was already frightened of Griffin, and she was terrified of what he would do if she told anyone about his vicious acts. She had to hope that Professor Mendoza would see the news story and put two and two together himself. She went on with her job search, anxious as ever to get out of Isla Colombo.

Later that evening Jerry Fenner was watching the eleven o'clock news. He was zoning out a bit amid the sweet smoke of his home-rolled reefer, but came to full attention when the Tollefson interview was replayed. *What does she mean it wasn't Brockton and they think they know who did it? Jesus Christ. Isn't Griffin keeping a lid on this? Did I fuck up somewhere?*

Fenner shut off the TV, finished his smoke and hit the sack.

CHAPTER 29

After Craig left the brew pub, Paul ordered and ate a burger for an early dinner, and then drove to the lab to find out if Carol Martin and the students had found anything in the plankton samples. Brad Barlow was in the lab and said that they had not found any evidence of jellyfish and that Dr. Martin had gone home.

Paul drove Brad to a McDonald's to pick up a burger for Brad, and they drove to the parking lot at Eighth Street to stake out the river bank. They swatted mosquitos in the shrubbery for four hours, but saw nothing more than a car with a young couple that parked and made out for a while. When the late-night surveillance shift arrived, Paul drove Brad to his car at the institute, and went home to his boat in Elk Rapids. The *Tondeleyo* had never been such a lonely place.

When Paul awoke Tuesday morning he remained lying on his back for a while staring up at the mahogany braces spanning the overhead. He was at a loss as to what to do first today, and what to do after that, and beyond—things seemed barely under control and not much progress was being made except for the MDEQ work at Whitetail Lake, and Paul did not have much to do with that other than watching from the sidelines. But of course the first order of business would be to visit Joan in the hospital again in hopes that there was some good news there. That got Paul off his bunk and into his usual jeans, RULI tee shirt and ball cap.

Unable to generate the energy to make breakfast, Paul drove up to River Street and had a full breakfast at the coffee shop. He brought a second coffee in a carry-out cup to the car and got onto U.S. 31 southward for Traverse City. The bright June day chipped away at his somber mood, and the intense blue of East Bay quickened his pulse. He was getting hopeful in spite of himself. Then his phone rang. *What now?*

"Is this Paul Tyson?" Paul's heart sank.

"Who is this?"

"This is Detective Parker."

This can't possibly be good. "What?"

"Can I meet with you this morning?"

"Um...I suppose so. What about your pal, Detective Baldwin is it?"

"Baldwin no longer works with me."

"Oh?"

"He's back to being a beat cop. We don't allow detectives to act the way he did in your lab. I have to apologize for that."

"Well I'll be damned."

"Yeah. Well, can we meet?"

"Yes. I would like Craig Basham to be in on it if you don't mind. I'm going to the hospital right now, and will probably see him there. I'll call you back to set something up."

"I'll be waiting. Thanks."

Paul drove on around the south end of the bay and over to the hospital. Craig was with the Brockton's in the lobby, and they did not look quite so forlorn this morning.

Mr. Brockton greeted Paul with a handshake. "Joan's pulmonary edema has subsided significantly since yesterday, and they don't need quite so much medication for her blood pressure. Urine production has picked up."

"Great to hear, Mr. Brockton."

"Call me Tom, will you? Anyway, she's still out completely, so the waiting goes on. But we're encouraged for the first time. Come on back to see her. If your words to her are any help, let's keep it up."

There was a hint of color in her face. Her heart monitor beeped in a steady cadence. Paul was able to speak to her with some hope in his voice, and he tried to convince himself he saw a glimmer of change in her expressionless face. *Was there some eyelid movement? Maybe not.*

Returning to the lobby Paul told Craig that the detective asked for a meeting and that Paul would like Craig to be there for that. Craig suggested that they meet in Craig's office. A law office setting might be a good thing. Paul called Parker and arranged to meet at Craig's office and gave him the address on Washington Street.

Chapter 30

Craig Basham's secretary announced the arrival of Detective Parker, and Craig told her to send him in. Another man accompanied Parker into Craig's office. Parker greeted Craig and Paul and shook their hands.

"You didn't tell me you were bringing a new partner," Paul said.

"Not exactly my new partner. Paul Tyson, Craig Basham, this is Special Agent Daniel Harkness, Homeland Security." Harkness was tall and fit with a ruddy complexion and light-brown short hair. He wore jeans and a blue blazer. Everyone shook hands.

"Why the surprise guest?" Paul asked Parker.

"I didn't want to freak you out over the phone," replied Parker. "I know you don't much care for law officers."

"I just don't like being bullied by them. I got enough of that two years ago."

"Yeah, I heard about that. We're not here for that. Dan happens to be a friend of mine, and I called him after you called me Saturday night. He came up from Detroit Sunday morning, and he's been busy ever since. As a result, we have become interested in your hunch about this Larry Griffin character. First of all, can you describe in more detail what he did here two years ago that would explain a motive for him?"

"Sure," said Paul. "In my blind fury over my false arrest for attempted murder of Ron Withers—I assume you have filled in Mr. Harkness about that whole fiasco—I stupidly got crosswise with Joan. Somewhere in there she accepted Griffin's invitation to go for a beer, and it got out of hand. He got her drunk and tried to get into her pants. When she refused, he threatened to give false testimony that he had seen me go below on the ship where Withers was fatally injured. She threw him out of her apartment. He did give the false testimony in court, but in the end it did not work. After the case was dropped he was fined for perjury, and later he was thrown out of the university for sexual harassment of a couple of his intro bio lab students. Joan's testimony helped accomplish that."

"Okay," said Parker. "That squares with what we've learned. Dan, you want to fill them in on the rest?"

Special Agent Harkness began. "Apparently Griffin did not begin his misogyny here. He was charged with rape at his undergrad college. He was not convicted, but he probably had a good lawyer and the girl probably didn't. There's also a record of problems when he was in high school, stuff like tying two neighborhood cats together, throwing the rope over a clothesline and watching them claw each other to death. His parents were both alcoholics. Typical story of a smart kid with a mean streak a mile wide. But we've lost track of him. Soon after he left the university he applied for and received a U.S. passport, and then he disappeared."

"We heard he got into a med school somewhere," said Paul. "Probably out of the country. So where do you stand now on Joan's involvement?"

"We brought in a genetics expert," said Parker. "We went through her lab with a fine-tooth comb and interviewed her doctoral advisor and student assistant. There is no evidence of any transgenic work there or anywhere else on this campus or anywhere else in northern Michigan. There is also no evidence that Ms. Brockton has traveled anywhere except to visit her parents in Farmington Hills near Detroit. So it's hard to see how she could have done the transgenic work. The DNA analysis of the hair in the lab book has not been completed, but even if it is hers, you are correct that it could have been planted there by someone. Dan?"

The special agent picked up the narrative. "As for how the animals and notebook got in her lab, we asked if there has been anyone unusual in the lab, and the student assistant said there was a plumber who came in to fix the gas line last Friday while Ms. Brockton was out; he had a large box, claiming it was a new gas spigot. We checked with the university maintenance department, and they have no record of any work like that being done. We obtained a copy of Griffin's passport and showed it to the student assistant, but she said it wasn't him."

"It wouldn't be," said Paul. "He's too smart for that. He's got someone working for him. Craig and I think it is the same person who is dumping fertilizer into the Boardman River, probably in a misguided plan to jack up the plankton biomass in the bay to feed the jellies he plans to plant there, if he hasn't already. We need to catch that guy; we've been watching the site where the dumping is being done to try to do that."

"You didn't tell me that," said Parker. "Where is the site?"

"At Eighth Street on the south side of the bridge, east side of the river. There's a parking lot there. We figure he does it at night."

"Yeah, I know that place. We should be helping with that. I assume there are things we can charge him with and hold him if we catch him?"

"Several state laws and county ordinances," replied Craig.

"Good. I'll get a car cruising by there."

"Make it an unmarked one; we don't want to spook him before he actually goes into the act. We might never see him again and he'll quit doing it."

"Gotcha. You have my number—call me the instant you see him carrying a bag to the river. Don't try to apprehend him yourselves. You may lose him that way too, and get hurt in the process. By the way, how are things going out at Whitetail Lake?"

"The MDEQ seems to have gotten control," Paul said.

"Good," said Parker as he stood up. "Gentlemen, we've got a plan. By the way, Paul, we've pulled the officer off of his vigil at the hospital."

They all stood up, and Parker and Harkness left Craig's office.

"Now we're getting somewhere," said Craig.

"I can't believe it. Good-cop-*good*-cop for a change. But a long way to go still. And Joan's not even close to being out of the woods even with Parker off her case for the time being."

Paul thanked Craig for hosting the meeting and left to go to his lab.

Paul drove to the institute and parked his Mustang in the usual place. As he walked to the limnology building he looked at the *Halcyon* sitting peacefully at her berth, her white pilothouse gleaming in the bright sun. He longed for the idyllic days when he and Joan went about their business doing good science and enjoying this magnificent bay area. Would she ever be with him doing that again? He trudged into the building a little less buoyant than he had been earlier in the day.

Dr. Perry told Paul that Brad Barlow was down the hall in Carol Martin's lab. Paul went there.

"No planulas so far," said Martin. She and her student and Barlow were sitting at microscopes. "We'll be done with yesterday's samples this afternoon."

"Good," said Paul. "Just in time to get some more. Tomorrow maybe?"

"You are a slave driver Paul. How is Joan?"

"Slightly better, I think." Paul went on to tell her and Brad the news of the meeting with Parker and Harkness in Basham's office."

"So we keep the pressure on at the river," said Brad.

"Yep," replied Paul.

CHAPTER 31

Juanita Salazar was doing some paperwork in the infirmary when she was startled by the arrival of Carlos, the custodian who had been stung by one of Larry Griffin's jellyfish.

"Can I help you Carlos?"

"I think my jellyfish stings have gotten infected." His fingers were swollen and weeping pus.

"Oh my, yes," said Juanita. She cleaned them and applied a topical antibiotic. "Are you allergic to penicillin?"

"No."

"Here is a package of tablets; take four a day for seven days, and come back then."

"Thank you," replied Carlos.

Juanita thought for a minute, and just as Carlos was leaving she called to him.

"Carlos, do you still clean in Dr. Mendoza's lab?"

"Yes."

"Do you know anything about what Larry Griffin is doing there?"

"No."

"Did they tell you that you were stung by a jellyfish that Griffin has made very dangerous with genes of an Australian species, the box jelly?"

"No. That is not good."

"You were very lucky that they could treat you quickly with the antidote. Please do not tell them that I am telling you this, okay Carlos?"

"Okay."

"I think Larry is doing some very bad things with this creation of his. Can you try to learn something about that without being caught?"

"I will try. What should I do?"

"Try to look at any notes on his desk, or things he has written in notebooks. But you will have to be very careful. Larry Griffin is a very mean man. Also, Dr. Mendoza does not want anyone to know about Larry's work either."

"I will try to find something."

"Thank you Carlos. Let me know if your hand gets worse during the next week. We might have to change to a different antibiotic."

After Carlos left the infirmary, Juanita ate her bag lunch, still trying to avoid Larry Griffin as much as possible. The rest of the day was uneventful, and while continuing to do paperwork she became increasingly anxious about Griffin. She had begun to stop thinking so much about him until today when Carlos came in. By the time she drove home at six o'clock she decided to call her brother. She could no longer keep it all to herself, no matter what her brother might say.

"Luis, can you come for dinner?"

"Sure, Juanita. What is wrong?"

"I didn't say anything is wrong."

"I hear it in your voice, little sister."

"Just come, please."

"I will be there in ten minutes."

After Carlos arrived they were silent as Juanita warmed up some quesadillas and served them with some Carib beer.

"It's time for you to talk to me, Juanita."

Juanita fought back tears. "I have some trouble and I am afraid."

"I'm listening Juanita. I am here for you. Just start at the beginning."

"I got involved with a man at the med school, an American student. I thought he was very handsome and charming. The charming part was only a trick. He became very bad."

Luis reddened and gripped the sides of the table. "Did he hurt you?"

"Not physically, but he humiliated me terribly. He did things I did not want him to do and swore at me when I resisted. He was so angry that I became afraid of him; that is why I moved to this apartment."

"Did he make you pregnant?"

"No. At least I don't think so. But I have sinned, Luis."

"Have you been to confession?"

"Yes."

"I do not care about your sinning. But I care about your fear of this man. Who is he? I will make him sorry he ever came here."

"You will do nothing of the sort, Luis. That's why I have been afraid to tell you. You will risk getting hurt, or arrested, or both. It is not worth that."

"Then what can I do?"

"Just give me moral support, and be ready to help if he ever tries to bother me again. But there is more going on. He has made a very dangerous transgenic jellyfish, a freshwater type that now has Australian box jelly genes that can kill people. I think he has somehow gotten it into lakes up in Michigan where he came from, and some people have been killed."

"Do you know this for sure?"

"No, but I think he is mean enough to do this. He is mad at some people there, and where else would the same transgenic jellyfish have come from? I am trying to learn more about this; a custodian at the school who also got hurt by them is spying in the lab for me."

"Okay, you are telling me to leave him alone, but you are pursuing his dangerous actions. Now I am telling *you* to leave him alone!"

"I just think someone must find out what he is doing. I think I can trust Carlos, the custodian, to keep me out of it."

"I don't like it. I want to at least stay here with you at night."

"He doesn't know where I live."

"He could find out. The university personnel office knows your address, right?"

"Well, yes. Okay. You can stay here. If you can stand sleeping on that couch."

"That is nothing."

Luis went to his boat to get some things.

The next afternoon Carlos was back in the infirmary to tell Juanita that his hand was already calming down, and that he already had some news for her.

"This morning I got a chance to look at Griffin's books and papers. Dr. Mendoza is away at a meeting in Cuba, and Griffin told me that since he was going to class it was a good time to mop the floors. There is a notebook right on his desk that is labeled 'Transgenic Freshwater Jellyfish,' and his name is on it. I read through it. I didn't understand much of it, but on the last page there was a man's name and address in Michigan; the man's last name was Fenner."

"You have done well, Carlos, thank you. I do not know what to do about this right now, but I will think of something. Please keep your eyes open and keep in touch with me. And be careful Carlos."

"I will."

CHAPTER 32

Wednesday morning it was overcast and drizzling in the Traverse Bay area when Paul was driving from his boat down to Traverse City. Paul had a sea bag with some extra clothes and a dopp kit with him. He had realized that he needed to be staying in Traverse while they were trying to catch the fertilizer dumper in the act, so that he could be on hand for that. He had gotten the Brockton's blessing to stay at Joan's studio apartment, since they were staying at Craig Basham's home where there was a full double bed in his guestroom; Joan had only a single daybed. The Brocktons were cooking some of their meals in Joan's apartment and using her shower, but Paul would just be sleeping there and not be in their way.

As usual the first stop of the day was the hospital. Joan's physiology was continuing to slowly improve, but she remained deeply comatose. Paul steadfastly continued speaking to her anyway. The Brocktons continued their vigil in the lobby.

At the institute later in the morning Paul and Brad Barlow took the *Chinook* out for some more plankton samples, this time working in foul weather gear in the light rain; at least the water was calm. Carol Martin stayed in her lab to get some other work done, as they didn't need three people for the sampling. She would help with the examination of the samples later in the day.

After returning the samples to Martin's lab, Paul and Brad went for lunch and then drove to Whitetail Lake to get some samples there to make sure larval jellies had not survived the rotenone treatment. The lake was a stinking mess, and MDEQ people were still raking in fish carcasses. No shotguns were necessary now; the few ducks that ventured near the lake surface must have caught the smell: every one of them veered off into the drizzly gloom and away to better places.

After finishing at Whitetail Lake, Paul and Brad visited four lakes near Whitetail Lake to sample them also. The MDEQ people were observing them to look for adult jellyfish, but Paul wanted to check for the planula larvae too. Returning to the institute, Paul and Brad joined Carol Martin and her student at the microscopes for a couple of hours, happily finding no evidence of jellyfish planulas. When they all stopped for the day, Paul called the county health department and gave an update of their findings to the environmental health division. Paul and Brad agreed to meet back at the lab after dinner to go set up their surveillance at the river.

Paul drove in the steady rain to the hospital to visit Joan and her parents again. Paul was happy to learn that the medical staff had begun to try to wean Joan off of the respirator, and she was making progress. After seeing Joan, Paul went to dinner with the Brocktons. They met at a waterfront restaurant on West Bay Shore Drive and got a table looking out at the bay. The rain had stopped, but fog was filling the still air and the sailboats sat ghostlike at their moorings. The mood was somber as their drinks arrived.

Mrs. Brockton took her first sip of her cocktail and set it down. "Paul, tell me about this man you suspect of doing this horrible thing. What would lead him, or drive him, to do such a thing? And why would Joan be such a target?"

Paul took a double swallow of his beer and thought for a minute or two. He decided to try to answer the second question first. He suspected that Joan hadn't told her parents about nearly being assaulted by Larry Griffin in her apartment two years ago, and therefore wasn't sure it was his place to talk about it. But with things so far out of hand now, he decided she would have told them by now if she could have.

"First of all, I have to say that Joan's involvement is largely my fault," Paul began. "She has probably not talked about this to you, and maybe she'll be unhappy with me if I do, but you deserve to know. Back when I got embroiled in the Ron Withers accident and was being prosecuted for suspected assault, I blew up at her for wondering if I could have actually done it, which was not an unreasonable thing for her to want to clear up given my state of nearly uncontrolled anger at the time. We withdrew from each other for a while, painfully for both of us, and she decided to escape a bit from a bad week in the lab and go drinking with Griffin. He's a handsome and persuasive guy.

"He managed to get a whole lot of beer into both of them, and she found herself alone with him in her apartment. She came to her senses and refused to cooperate when he started to get physical. When he threatened to falsely testify against me unless she slept with him, she threw him out. He was apparently very humiliated, not used to being rejected. But worse than that for him, Joan testified against him later in a sexual harassment case that got him thrown out of the university."

The Brocktons nodded and then shook their heads. "So he has carried a pretty big grudge since then," said Mrs. Brockton. "But why such vicious, murderous action? He's an educated and supposedly civilized man."

"Now we are out of my depth; I'm no psychologist," replied Paul. "But he does have a prior record of violence; he apparently raped a girl in undergrad school although escaped conviction, and did some vicious things to neighborhood pets as a kid. There must be something in his past that has shut off his civility genes and turned on the violent ones. Perhaps if we ever get to him we can learn what that was, but until then we'll never know. Of course we still don't even know if he really is involved here. But this thing has his name written all over it."

"I agree," said Mr. Brockton.

Their meal arrived, and they ate mostly in silence. The Brocktons left for Craig Basham's house and Paul left to return to the lab.

CHAPTER 33

Back at the lab, Brad Barlow had returned from going to dinner with Dr. Martin's student, and was waiting for Paul. Although it was early in the evening and ordinarily it would still be quite a while until darkness, the fog had continued to build and it was much darker than usual. Paul decided they should go on over to the river at Eighth Street to lie in wait for the fertilizer dumper. It was getting frustrating, all those nights of hiding uncomfortably in wait. But it was their only way to make the potential connection to Larry Griffin.

"I hope the rain has stopped for good," said Paul. "We're certainly not going to sit around out there hiding in bright yellow foul weather gear. Let's go."

They drove through the thick fog south on Boardman Avenue and pulled into the parking lot next to the Eighth Street bridge. They parked in front of the building that was alongside the river. There were a few other cars in the lot but they were empty and no one was around. They got out and walked around to the shrubbery next to the building where they could see the lot and the seawall along the river. But they couldn't see very well in the fog.

"Good night for a dumping operation, if you don't want to be seen," said Paul.

"Sure is," replied Brad. "Maybe we'll get lucky tonight."

The hours went by like they were dragging anchors, and Paul and Brad didn't seem to be getting lucky. They were stiff and cramped in the chilly fog, and looking forward to the arrival of the late shift of people that were volunteering for Craig Basham. Then at eleven fifteen a white pickup truck slowly emerged out of the fog, turning off of Eighth Street onto Boardman Avenue and into the parking lot. It rumbled right up close to the shrubbery where Paul and Brad were and parked.

Paul's pulse quickened in fear that the truck was so close that they would be discovered. It quickened more when he realized it was a white Ford F150. A white F150 was burned into his memory from Jake Fenner's three-month-long harassment of him two years ago culminating in Fenner's attempt to run Paul and Joan down and killing himself in the ensuing wreck. Here, the driver got out of the truck and walked around to the truck bed. Paul thought he was seeing the ghost of Jake Fenner. Same long greasy hair, same crummy tee shirt. *This can't be happening.* Then Paul remembered that Jake Fenner had a younger brother. *Oh my god. Is this Griffin's connection? Of course.* Paul got a hold of himself and started getting a video clip going with his smartphone, hoping it would work in all this fog. *Damn good thing he is so close to us.*

Jerry Fenner pulled a large sack out of the truck bed, threw it over his shoulder, and walked over to the river's edge.

"Sneak out and get the license number in case we lose him," Paul whispered to Brad. "But be careful."

While Brad was reading the license plate, Fenner ripped open the bag and dumped its contents into the river. Brad got back behind the shrubbery just as Fenner turned back toward the truck. Fenner got another bag of fertilizer out of the truck and took it to the river. Paul wanted to call Detective Parker now, but Fenner was so close to them that Paul was afraid Fenner would hear him talking. All they could do was wait until Fenner finished and got back in his truck.

Fenner threw the two empty bags in the truck bed, got in the cab and started the noisy engine. Paul immediately dialed Detective Parker's cell phone.

"This is Tyson. We got the bastard."

"What do you mean?"

"He just dumped two bags of fertilizer into the river here at Eighth Street. I think I got it on video. He's pulling out of the parking lot now. We're going to follow him. White F-one-fifty pickup. Can you get rolling?"

"Absolutely. And I'll radio the dispatcher to get a backup officer rolling. Stay on the phone and tell me which way he's headed."

Paul and Brad ran for the Mustang and got in. Paul handed Brad his cell phone and started the car. When the truck turned left from Boardman Avenue onto Eighth Street headed east, Paul backed up and pulled out of the parking lot.

"Brad, tell Parker that the truck is headed east on Eighth, and that we are following it." Brad did so. He told Paul he could hear Parker radioing that information to the backup cruiser that was approaching the area.

The truck's taillights were already lost in the fog, and Paul speeded up a little, even though he was afraid of getting too close. Finally he saw the truck. Fortunately Fenner was not driving fast, and Paul could drive at a safe speed without following too closely. After seven blocks that seemed to Paul like dozens, the truck stopped at Garfield with its right turn signal on.

"Tell Parker he's turning south on Garfield." Brad did so.

"Also recommend that they not use flashers or sirens, at least not yet; I don't want to spook this guy." Brad did so.

Before Paul could turn right himself, another car came out of the gloom through the intersection and was now behind the truck. Paul completed the turn. It would be harder to keep an eye on Fenner, but Paul figured at least his

Mustang would be masked by the new arrival. After a mile or so Paul saw a car approaching behind him. He thought he could see a police light bar across the top of it; if that was what it was, it was not flashing. *Good.*

"Brad, use your own phone and call Craig Basham and tell him what's happening and to start coming this way; we'll keep him informed of where we end up." Paul dictated Craig's number, and Brad made the call.

The parade of vehicles proceeded for several more miles, and then slowed way down to a crawl. Paul could see the left turn signal of the truck blinking.

"Brad, tell Parker the truck is turning left into the entrance of a trailer park. Ask him if he is with us behind the cruiser that is right behind us." Brad spoke to Parker on Paul's phone.

"Parker says he is with us, and they will follow us in behind the truck, but if the guy gets spooked, we should pull over and let Parker and the backup pursue."

"Okay," said Paul. "Keep telling Craig where we are. The sign at the entrance said 'Garfield Downs.'"

The car in front of Paul impatiently pulled onto the gravel shoulder and passed to the right of the truck as Fenner slowly made his left turn into the trailer park. Paul let the truck proceed for a few dozen yards and then followed in behind it; the two county cruisers slowly followed behind Paul with their headlights off. Fenner drove straight eastward on the main thoroughfare past a couple of dozen single-wides until the old potholed road came to a T, where he turned right. Paul hesitated at the corner, not wanting to be too obvious. He watched the truck turn into the gravel parking space beside the third trailer on the left; Paul then quickly pulled around the corner and stopped just beyond Fenner's trailer. The light bar came to life on the backup cruiser as it pulled in behind Paul's car and blocked in the truck. Detective Parker stopped behind the flashing cruiser at an angle facing the white truck and turned on his headlights.

Jerry Fenner emerged from his truck cab and squinted in the glare of Parker's headlights, his pale face reflecting the pulsing blue lights from the backup cruiser. The uniformed officer approached Fenner with his hand on the butt of his Glock, with Parker in jeans and sweatshirt a few steps behind and to the side.

"I haven't gone over thirty-five all night," said Fenner. "What's the deal?"

"Just put your hands on your truck and spread your feet," said Parker.

"Hey, I got no drugs or nuthin'. Why are you shakin' me down like this?"

The backup officer patted Fenner down and then brought his arms behind him and cuffed him. The officer pulled Fenner's cell phone from his front pocket, and then pulled his wallet out of his back pocket and looked at his driver's license. Paul and Brad were walking toward the arrest scene now, and they heard the officer say Fenner's name: "Gerald Fenner."

"Nobody calls me Gerald, man. It's Jerry."

Paul's hunch that this was Jake Fenner's brother was confirmed. Paul nodded slowly and then saw Craig Basham's Ford Escape pull up behind Parker's cruiser.

"What are all these fertilizer bags doing in your truck?" Parker asked Fenner.

"Got to tend my lawn."

Everyone looked over at the small dry patch of stunted weedy grass next to Fenner's rusty gray trailer, and back at Fenner.

"I work landscape and lawn service, man."

"Where?" asked Parker.

"Here, there and everywhere. Freelance, you know."

By now Craig Basham had joined the group and was listening. Parker took Basham aside and asked him, "What are those environmental laws we are arresting him for?" Craig cited a few of them. Parker turned back to Fenner."

"You're under arrest for violation of a county ordinance and two state anti-pollution laws. You were observed dumping two of these bags of fertilizer into the Boardman River about twenty minutes ago." Parker read Fenner his Miranda rights.

"You gotta be kidding, man. Musta been someone else. It's dark and foggy. I was just drivin' home from work."

"These two gentlemen watched you do it in the parking lot at Eighth and Boardman and followed you here," said Parker.

"Who the hell are you?" Fenner snarled at Paul and Brad.

"Your worst nightmare, pal," replied Paul.

"You didn't see shit, buddy."

"Shit's a good word for what we saw, and it was you. My cell phone saw it too; you're a video star."

"The video can't be worth a damn—too foggy. I'm tellin' you it wasn't me."

Paul took a deep breath and pulled out his phone. He hadn't had a chance to view the video, and wasn't at all sure it was any good. He ran it for himself first, and smiled. He showed it to Detective Parker, who nodded.

"You're busted pal," said Parker to Fenner. "Can we take a look in your trailer?"

"No," said Fenner. "Get a warrant. I wanna see a lawyer."

"In due time," replied Parker. "Right now you're coming downtown."

"Hey Fenner," said Paul. "Jake was your brother, right?"

Fenner did a double take with bulging eyes at Paul. "Who the hell *are* you, asshole?"

Paul stared back.

"Oh Christ," said Fenner. "You're that Tyson puke."

"Your brother missed me."

"Damn shame."

"You know someone by the name of Larry Griffin?"

"Who?" said Fenner, suddenly having a coughing fit.

"Larry Griffin."

Fenner got control. "Never heard of him."

"We'll see about that."

Detective Parker helped the uniformed officer load Fenner into the backseat of the officer's cruiser and said he would join them at headquarters shortly. Paul pulled his Mustang out of the way so that the cruiser could leave with Fenner. Parker, Paul and Craig went over to take a look at Fenner's truck. There were several full bags of fertilizer in the back and some empty bags among them; nothing else. Parker opened the unlocked cab door and shined a flashlight around in there. He saw nothing at first, and the glove compartment was empty. But behind the right-hand seat he pulled out an empty cardboard box with a FedEx shipping label on it.

"Lookee here," said Parker.

"It's addressed to Fenner," said Paul. He looked at the number on Fenner's mailbox; it was the same as on the package.

"It is from someplace called Isla Colombo; no sender's name, just a P.O. box number. But now we're getting somewhere," said Paul. He pulled out his smartphone, opened his Internet browser and Googled Isla Colombo. In less than two minutes he found the web site for the Medical College of Isla Colombo.

"Bingo," said Paul. "There's a med school there. It's in the Caribbean. Griffin is in med school. The web site does not list current students' names, but they do have a gene technology program and a professor that does transgenics. I think we have a smoking gun here. What is the next step with Fenner?"

"I will go to the county jail and attempt to interrogate him further, but it looks like he will refuse to discuss anything without a lawyer, which I doubt he has nor can afford. That means waiting to get him a court-appointed attorney. That will take us through most of tomorrow I imagine. Same for getting a court order to search his house."

Craig Basham entered the conversation. "We need to credibly establish his connection with Fenner as soon as possible so we can charge him with more than pollution activity; you're not going to be able to hold him very long otherwise. If Fenner is involved with Griffin, there has probably been telephone contact. Can you pursue that angle quickly?"

"I'll get Dan working on that," said Parker.

"That's your friend the Homeland Security agent, right?"

"Yep."

"Good," said Basham. "Make sure Fenner doesn't get off any calls to Griffin that would warn him that we are on his trail."

"Yep," replied Parker. "Okay, I'd better get going. I'll see you guys tomorrow. Thanks for the good work, Tyson."

"Thanks for taking over so quickly," replied Paul.

Detective Parker took the FedEx box to his cruiser and drove off in the gloom. Craig Basham agreed to meet Paul at the Sheriff's headquarters at ten tomorrow, and drove off for home. Paul and Brad Barlow got in Paul's Mustang for the trip back into town, where Paul dropped Brad off at his car in the institute lot and then drove to Joan's apartment for the night.

CHAPTER 34

By Wednesday morning the fog had cleared off, and the day was partly cloudy and warm. Paul dressed in his usual jeans and RULI tee shirt, and ate a hardboiled egg from Joan's fridge and some cereal. He got a coffee at a coffee shop near the apartment building and drove to the hospital.

Joan's parents were not in the lobby this time, and Paul didn't know quite what to do. A little worried, he walked to the nurses' station near the ICU to ask about them. Mrs. Brockton was just then coming out of the ICU.

"Hi Paul. You might as well come right on in."

Paul did not know quite what to think of this, and got even more worried. They went through the door and approached Joan, who was lying there as she had been doing for days. But Paul could see her breathing.

"So what is the latest from the doctors?" Paul asked Mrs. Brockton, who glanced over at Joan. Paul followed her glance and saw Joan's eyelids flicker and then open.

"Hi Paul."

Paul was so stunned his vision blurred for a moment and he swayed into Mr. Brockton, who caught him and held on until Paul regained his equilibrium.

"Joanie. You're back." He reached for her hand and bent to kiss her. She smiled and squeezed his hand, but her squeeze was barely perceptible.

"Partway, anyway. My hands don't work too well and I can't move my legs."

Paul's refused to let that news destroy the joy of seeing her awake and talking to him.

"I heard you talking to me, Paul. I was determined to come back."

"Never a doubt, Joan," he lied. "And you're going to come the rest of the way back." He wished that he was as confident as he was trying to sound. There was still no way of knowing how much neurological damage had been done, and how much of it was reversible. He knew she knew that by the tear that rolled down her cheek, but she was still smiling.

"I don't remember anything," Joan said. "But they tell me I was stung by a transgenic jellyfish. I don't understand."

"We're all working very hard to get that figured out, and we will fill you in when we know more and when you are stronger. You just keep working on getting better."

Paul stayed a while longer and reassured Joan that her lab and her teaching duties were being taken care of and that her apartment was fine too. He chose not to discuss the situation with Jerry Fenner and the probable Griffin connection yet. He gave her another kiss and said he would be in every day to see her.

Chapter 35

Paul drove from the hospital to the county sheriff's headquarters reeling between joy at Joan's coming out of the coma and dread that she would remain paralyzed for the rest of her life. He renewed his determination that Griffin, whom he was now certain had done this to Joan and killed those two kids, would pay for this. He found Craig Basham sitting in the lobby waiting for him.

"Good news and bad news," said Craig.

"First, I have some of both for you," Paul interrupted. He told Craig that Joan had finally come awake and was lucid, but that her legs were paralyzed and arms were weak.

Craig smiled broadly at the good news and winced at the bad news. "I have to believe that she will continue improving," he said.

"Amen. Now what is your news?"

"Agent Dan Harkness has learned some things. First of all, he has learned that over the past year Baines Biological Supply has shipped several orders of freshwater jellyfish to the med school in Isla Colombo. But Larry Griffin was not the person on the order; it was to the lab of a Dr. Mendoza."

"Yep, that's the transgenic guy," said Paul. "Griffin must be working in that lab."

"But no evidence of that as of now," said Craig. "There's more good and bad news. The phone call log in Fenner's cell phone shows calls from Larry Griffin's phone."

"Bingo again. That is huge," said Paul.

"Yes, but here's the problem. It is a phone number of Griffin's originating here in our Traverse City area code. He has not gotten a new account wherever he is now; certainly not Isla Colombo. He must have an international service component, or else Isla Colombo has roaming capability for the U.S. system. But we can't show a definite connection of Griffin to Isla Colombo yet."

"Damn," said Paul. "Can't Harkness find him down there? Maybe through this Mendoza guy?"

"Apparently Mendoza is out of the country right now, and the college won't reveal student names. Dan has also done some checking about Isla Colombo. Because of some nasty lawsuits by our feds against a couple of shady banks down there, the Isla Colombo government has become totally uncooperative with the U.S. They're denying him entry into the country to investigate the college, and they have a policy of not extraditing anyone from Isla Colombo to the U.S. even if we do locate Griffin."

"More brick walls. How about a covert operation?"

"Harkness doesn't think that Homeland Security will give our situation high enough priority for that, but he's checking."

"And what's the status of getting a warrant to search Fenner's trailer?" asked Paul.

"They already have it, and Parker and Harkness are out there now. I guess we just wait to hear from them."

Paul and Craig sat and chatted for a half hour, got some lousy coffee from a machine in the lobby, and chatted for another half hour. Then Craig's phone rang.

"This is Basham. Uh huh. Uh huh. Really? Holy shit. Amazing. Don't open the damn thing—just bring it back and Paul will know what to do with it. Okay, we'll be here."

Paul was nearly apoplectic waiting to learn what the hell Craig was hearing.

"Dude, they didn't even need the warrant," said Craig to Paul. "A FedEx package from Isla Colombo was sitting on

Fenner's doorstep addressed to him. It contains a Baines Biological carton, two thousand bucks, and a note that says 'Here's the final installment. Dump this one in the bay near the river mouth. Then you're done buddy—good job.' It's signed L.G."

"Bingo. Got both the bastards!"

"Well, L.G. is not enough to clearly implicate Griffin yet. But they can charge Fenner with murder and hold him indefinitely while we work on tying in Griffin for sure. We do have to verify that there are transgenic jellies in the carton."

"We can do that pretty quickly," said Paul. "And we can report that the things have not been put in the bay yet; the chamber of commerce will be glad to hear that."

"Yep."

Chapter 36

Fifteen minutes later Detective Parker and Agent Harkness walked into the lobby with the FedEx package and signaled to Paul and Craig to follow them into his office down the hall. Parker showed Paul and Craig the contents of the FedEx package, and also showed them the notes that they found in Fenner's trailer with instructions about the fertilizer dumping and about what to do with the things that Griffin had sent earlier including the Baines cartons, the trumped-up data notebook, and the anonymous note to the police.

"Okay," said Parker. "We have enough to charge Fenner with two counts of murder and one count of attempted murder. I will file that immediately. I'm going to try to get him to talk about Griffin—we still don't have Griffin's name or prints or DNA on anything—but Fenner will probably keep stalling till he gets a lawyer. We may have to end up plea bargaining to get testimony against Griffin. But as you know, we will have trouble getting Griffin out of Isla Colombo because of their non-extradition policy. Unless because he is American they won't care about protecting him. I doubt that though—they're unlikely to want to cooperate at all, they're so pissed at us about our attack on their banks. Now Dan here wants to confirm that there are transgenic jellies in this carton. Can you help with that, Paul?"

"Yes," replied Paul. "Let's take them to the lab."

Craig Basham stayed at the police station to monitor the proceedings with Fenner while Agent Harkness took the Baines Biological carton to his car and followed Paul's Mustang to the institute. Paul and Harkness parked next to each other and went in to the Perry lab with the carton. Paul saw that Dr. Perry was in his office, and explained to him what was going on. Perry came into the lab to watch Paul work with the carton of jellyfish.

"Be careful with those damn things, Paul."

"Absolutely," replied Paul.

Paul laid a plastic-backed absorptive pad on a lab bench and put the Baines carton on it. He pulled on a pair of vinyl gloves and carefully opened the carton. There they were, gently undulating around in the water. Paul filled a beaker with water and transferred a jellyfish into it with a pair of forceps. He invited Perry and Harkness to follow him into the equipment room where he turned off the lights. Sure enough, the jelly glowed in the dark.

"This is the real deal. Griffin included a gene for bioluminescence in the package of genes he transferred from the box jelly as a 'reporter gene' to make it easy for him to tell if the transfer worked. But we need to test the actual toxicity of these things. Let's go back into the main room and I'll make a phone call."

Paul called a postdoc he knew in a genetics lab and asked if they had any lab mice that had finished serving in an experiment and were going to be sacrificed soon. Yes they did, and Paul was welcome to one of the untreated controls. Paul went next door to the biology building to get one. With scissors they clipped some fur to make an area of bare skin on the mouse's back, and Paul brought the mouse back to his lab. He picked the jellyfish out of the beaker with forceps and prepared to lay it on the mouse's bare back.

"If it's not a transgenic, nothing will happen," said Paul. "The native jellies are harmless to mammals. If it's transgenic, he'll die almost instantly. A sad but necessary sacrifice to find out for sure."

"Wait a second," said Harkness. "I want to get a video of this. Start with a new one out of the carton." He pulled out his smartphone and started recording a video of the Baines carton, and told Paul to go ahead.

Paul picked a jelly out of the carton and put it on the mouse's bare back. The mouse arched its back, stiffened, fought for breath, and slowly slumped back down. It was dead within ninety seconds. The jellyfish was definitely transgenic. Paul put the dead mouse in a Ziplock bag and took it back to the genetics lab, asked them to dispose of it according to their normal disposal protocol, and thanked them. Returning to the Perry lab, he asked Agent Harkness what they should do next.

"Is there any way we can keep these things alive for a while?" asked Harkness. "They'll be needed for evidence, if that's possible."

"I'll call Linda Carter and see if she could help with that. She keeps the normal ones in her prep room for the intro bio labs."

He made the call, explained what was going on, and Linda agreed to keep them alive as long as she could. Paul closed the carton and he and Harkness took it next door to the biology building and up to Linda's prep room. She didn't need to be warned to keep them locked away from anyone who might inadvertently come in contact with them. Harkness and Paul thanked her, left the biology building and returned to the Perry Lab.

"Dan," said Paul, "I think we should keep our knowledge of the Griffin connection out of the news for now so that he doesn't do anything to cover his tracks down there and go into hiding or anything. In fact, it would be nice to keep everything we've learned out of the news, but I suppose that is impossible. The city needs to know that this thing is largely solved and under control now. Even without mention of Griffin in the news I'm afraid that if Griffin hears about it he will fear that Fenner will rat him out on a plea bargain, but what can we do?"

"I'm sure Parker will agree that talking about Griffin to the press is premature; we don't have enough to legally implicate him yet anyway."

"So what about a covert action to get Griffin when we can implicate him?"

"Covert actions often don't stay covert, especially after they happen, and Homeland Security—or really the CIA—will be unlikely to want to start an international incident over this, especially now that we have wiped out Griffin's operation at this end and are alert to anything he may try in the future. In other words the danger of continued damage by him is extremely low now, so he's no bin Laden."

"So we wait for him to re-enter the U.S. to get hold of him, right?"

"Yep."

"I don't like that."

"Join the club. Well, I need to get back to headquarters to fill Parker in on what we found here. Thanks for your help, Paul."

"Likewise to you, Dan."

CHAPTER 37

After Agent Harkness left the lab, Paul and Dr. Perry went up to Director Tollefson's office to fill her in on the latest information about Fenner and the Griffin connection. She was delighted to hear that they had nailed Fenner and that the greater Traverse City community seemed to be out of danger now.

"We still have to monitor the lakes and ponds around Whitetail Lake to make sure the jellies haven't gotten transferred into them," said Paul.

"Of course. But I want to bring the mayor and the chamber of commerce up to date, both to reassure the public and the tourist businesses and to allay their suspicions of Joan and the institute."

"Certainly," said Paul. "But can you leave Griffin's name out of it for now? We don't have good legal evidence that he is behind all of this, and we want to avoid spooking him into hiding before we can get at him. That bastard needs to pay, excuse my French."

"French, eh? Well, 'bastard' is 'skitstövel' in Swedish, which is what I would call him, in addition to some other things."

"You never cease to amaze me, Dr. Tollefson."

"You can call me Karen, Paul, as long as you use the Swedish pronunciation—which I haven't been able to get anyone else here to do." Tollefson looked pointedly at Dr. Perry and pronounced her name again with the broad "aah" sound. "Now, what are the plans to make that skitstövel pay?"

"None at the moment," replied Paul, unable to bring himself to use Tollefson's first name. And he did not want to express the thoughts that had begun to crop up in the back of his mind during the past few hours about dealing with Griffin. But those thoughts were beginning to work their way to the front of his mind.

"Okay," said Tollefson. "Thank you both for getting me up to date. I will call the mayor right away."

Paul and Dr. Perry went back down to the lab. Brad Barlow was there now, and they filled him in on all of the latest news.

"Thanks again for all of your help in smoking out Fenner," said Paul. "And for your hard work in monitoring for the jellies. That part has to continue, because we can't be sure they haven't been transferred into other lakes. Can you keep that up for a while?"

"Sure," replied Brad. "Glad to help. By the way, all of this has gotten me really interested in limnology, and I like working with Dr. Martin. I'm thinking of joining her lab if she'll accept me."

"Well," said Dr. Perry, "if I weren't retired, I'd try to compete to have you stay here, but Dr. Martin is a great choice for you, and she will be fortunate to have you."

"Thanks, Dr. Perry."

Paul cleaned up the materials he had used for the toxicity test, and then called Craig Basham who was still at police headquarters. Paul learned that Detective Parker and Agent Harkness were still interrogating Jerry Fenner, probably with their best good-cop-bad-cop act. Paul drove to the station, and he and Craig walked to a restaurant for lunch.

Chapter 38

In the interrogation room at police headquarters, Parker and Harkness were getting nowhere with Jerry Fenner. As Parker was asking Fenner for the hundredth time who the "L.G." on the notes in Fenner's trailer was, there was a knock on the door.

"Come in," shouted Parker.

It was a uniformed officer. "The court appointed attorney is here."

"Who is it?" asked Parker.

"Darnell Gates," replied the officer.

"Wait a minute," said Fenner. "That sounds like the name of a 'brother,' if you know what I mean. I don't want no 'brother' fuckin' up my case."

"Fenner, you're a stupid asshole," said Parker. "Gates has the best record of all the public defenders in Grand Traverse County for successfully defending jerks like you. Nobody wins 'em all, but he wins more than most."

"With white guys too?"

"White guys too."

Fenner groaned. "Okay, send the sumbitch in."

Parker rolled his eyes, shook his head, and then motioned to the officer to bring in the strikingly handsome attorney, who was dressed in a brown suit, blue shirt, and a tie with a vaguely African pattern on it.

"Mr. Gates, how are you," said Parker as he rose to shake hands with the attorney.

"Fine, Detective Parker. This is Mr. Fenner, I presume?"

"This is Mr. Gerald Fenner, who is eager for your services."

Gates looked at the scowling redneck and said, "I'll bet he is. Well you gentlemen can leave us alone if you please."

Parker, Harkness and the uniformed officer left the room.

Darnell Gates sat down opposite Fenner and opened the folder containing information about Fenner, the circumstances of his arrest, and the charges against him. Fenner still had his scowl.

"Mr. Fenner, you don't look happy to see me. Nothing new to me. But let's get this straight. You don't have to like me and I don't have to like you. I am paid to give you the best legal advice I can and make sure you are treated fairly, whether you deserve it or not. My goal is to succeed and I work very hard to do that, not because I want to please my clients but because I want to enhance my career. I don't intend to be a public defender forever."

"Okay Mr. Gates," replied Fenner. "Let's get on with it then."

"Okay. Mr. Fenner, I have to put it to you straight. They have you in a pretty tight bind. They've got good evidence that somebody named 'L.G.' sent you some things including some very dangerous animals and paid you to put them in places where people were in danger of getting killed, and two kids did get killed by them. They saw you dump fertilizer bags in the river, which didn't kill anyone, but it was part of the instructions from L.G. They showed your mug shot to a student working in Miss Brockton's lab, and she identified you as the man who was in her lab masquerading as a plumber with a package you left on Ms. Brockton's desk the day before Brockton was critically stung, which was also part of L.G.'s instructions, and the university denies that you work for them or for anyone they have contracted. And I can't find any evidence that they screwed up their investigation or arrest in any way that can be used as a defense on technical grounds. As is stands right now, you face indictment and conviction for first degree murder which in Michigan carries a mandatory life sentence."

Fenner frowned and thought for a minute. "Is it true that anything I say to you stays with you?"

"That's the law."

"You stick by that?"

"I do."

"L.G. is Larry Griffin. He never told me people would die. Just get annoyed and maybe hurt some. I never would have done it if I'd a known people would die. I'm not a killer; I just wanted some extra money, and maybe I did have a grudge against Brockton's boyfriend. But I didn't want nobody dead."

"Well, saying you didn't know the things were lethal could help a little if they were to believe you. But do they know about your grudge against Brockton's boyfriend? What's his name?"

"Tyson. They can probably figure it out. My brother was killed after tangling with him."

"Did the guy kill your brother?"

"No. My brother just got careless trying to fuck up Tyson. Twice. The second time he and his buddy died when his truck missed Tyson and Brockton and crashed into the bay.

"But you do have a motive of sorts."

"I guess so."

"What was Griffin's motive?"

"He was after Brockton and the university. I don't really know much about that."

"Well look. With the evidence they have you are likely to be indicted as at least an accessory to first degree murder. I assume it will be obvious that there's no way you could have engineered those lethal animals yourself, and I can believe that you didn't know that people would die and a jury might believe you too, but if you are indicted I'm afraid the only way to make sure you avoid a conviction and a life sentence will be to accept a plea bargain and testify against this Griffin. Where is he?"

"He is on a Caribbean island somewhere."

"Oh yes. It says here the packages came from Isla Colombo. Oh boy. They don't extradite Americans there."

"What's that mean?"

"They won't send him back here for trial."

"Then will a plea bargain still work for me?"

"It should. Parker and Harkness will just wait for him to enter the U.S. eventually."

"And what would I get?"

"Probably fifteen years or less for manslaughter, with possibility of early release. That's what my deal with them would be. I would bargain for five."

"I'll think about it. Griffin will be after my ass if I do it, and you see what the fucker can do."

"That's a risk, but hopefully he would eventually be in prison for the rest of his life. So think about it. Anyway, you will plead not guilty to the charge of first degree murder at your arraignment, which will be tomorrow at ten a.m. I'll be here at nine-thirty."

Gates collected the folder of papers and rose to tell the officers he was finished for now.

Chapter 39

Paul and Craig returned to police headquarters after lunch. They learned from Detective Parker that Fenner's court appointed attorney had met with Fenner, that the arraignment would be tomorrow at ten, and that Fenner would not be talking to anyone until after a grand jury decision is handed down, probably in a week or so.

"So we still don't have Griffin implicated by Fenner," said Parker. "His attorney probably does now, but of course he will keep that under attorney-client privilege, and will likely use it in a plea bargain after the grand jury indicts Fenner."

"Is an indictment pretty certain?" asked Paul.

"I think so, and I think Gates, the attorney, thinks so too."

"But no Griffin action for now."

"Nope."

"Shit."

"Yep."

Craig Basham left to return to his office to attend to the volumes of paperwork that he had been putting off for days while embroiled in the jellyfish holocaust, and Paul left to return to the lab at the institute.

Parking his Mustang in the institute lot, he walked out onto the dock beside the *Halcyon*. Things had sort of ground to a halt, and after days of just reacting to one event after another he relished the chance to sit down and think about things. He boarded the *Halcyon,* climbed the ladder to the boat deck, and sat down on the deck between the lifeboat and the lifelines on the port side facing east. With little wind the sun had heated up the day, but Paul was in the shade of the lifeboat and comfortable. He could see the plankton bloom along the shore and was pleased to know that, now that Fenner would not be dumping any more fertilizer, the bloom would eventually subside and the bay would return to normal. Whitetail Lake would take longer to recover, but it would recover. But what about Joan? A gloom of pessimism flooded in along with renewed anger at Larry Griffin for doing this to her. Would she ever walk again, and get back to her brilliant dissertation work, and sail with Paul and share the other things that they did together? *That son of a bitch sits down there on that island completely immune to the justice he deserves. Well, maybe not completely immune.*

Paul sat for a time trying to enjoy the pleasant scene before him while a plan began to take shape. By mid-afternoon he stood up, went back down onto the dock and walked to the lab in the limnology building. He found his passport in his file cabinet and checked that it was nowhere near expiring. He had no idea whether he could get into Isla Colombo with it, but in any case a passport was now required to enter St. Thomas even though it is a U.S. territory. He got on his computer and accessed the Delta Airlines web site. He was able to book a trip to St. Thomas leaving tomorrow morning. There was just no time to lose before Griffin wised up and disappeared, and no one else was going to do a damn thing about it. There would be plane changes both in Detroit and in Atlanta—a pain in the butt, but so be it. Paul booked the trip with his credit card.

Paul told Dr. Perry that he was going to be away from the lab for a couple of days; Perry was hard at work on a grant review in his office and simply nodded his acknowledgement of Paul's comment, seemingly without attaching any particular significance to it, which suited Paul perfectly. *Hope it will be that easy to tell everyone else about this.* Paul went to find Brad Barlow in Carol Martin's lab. Brad was there, and Paul told him he would be away for a few days, and asked him to keep up the monitoring of the lakes around Whitetail Lake. Thankfully Brad did not seem curious about Paul's plans either.

Chapter 40

Paul left the building, drove to Joan's apartment and packed his sea bag with the few things he had there, and then drove to the hospital.

Mr. Brockton was in the ICU lobby and greeted Paul with a broad smile.

"Some good news, Paul. They will be moving Joan out of the ICU tomorrow. She doesn't need all of the tubes and wires and contraptions there anymore."

"Fantastic," said Paul. "How is her movement coming along?"

"Arms moving now, though weakly. No legs yet. We're hopeful. They're starting physical therapy tomorrow too."

"Tom, I have to bring you up to date. I don't know how much you have told Joan yet, but working with the law officers we have caught the guy who was dumping fertilizer in the river and learned that he is the one who put the lethal jellies in the lake and on Joan's desk. It was by direction of that bastard Larry Griffin, who made them transgenic at a med school on Isla Colombo in the Caribbean and FedExed them to Jerry Fenner. Fenner is the younger brother of Jake Fenner who was killed in his truck when he tried to ram Joan and me two years ago."

"My god. This is unbelievable. But it does make sense, in a twisted way."

"So what do we tell Joan?"

"She is ready to hear it all, I think. It will be better than her wondering with no clue—the more alert and contemplative she gets the more not knowing anything is driving her crazy. And she is a tough gal, as you well know."

"Okay. One more thing. They don't have anything more than circumstantial evidence of Griffin's role; Fenner is not talking to anyone but his lawyer, and probably won't until and if he makes a plea bargain, which would be at least a week from now. And Homeland Security won't make a move on Griffin even just to get evidence down there because of the political situation with Isla Colombo. He's likely to figure out what we know very soon and cover his tracks. Sooo...let me put it this way, I am going to be gone for a few days. I'm not saying where or why, so that no one has to feel compelled to either tell the authorities if asked, or to lie to them."

"Jesus Paul. I hope you know what you are doing. Joan doesn't need to have you involved in a tragedy too."

"Well, I really already have been, with her in there having narrowly escaped death and still paralyzed. I just cannot sit around here and do nothing about this."

"All right. Be careful Paul. Let's go in and see her."

Paul and Mr. Brockton walked down the hall into Joan's room.

"Hey Joanie," said Paul. "I hear they're pulling all this claptrap off of you and putting you to work with the physical therapists."

"Yep," she said with a grin.

"Do you know what slave drivers they are?"

"Yep."

Mr. Brockton motioned to his wife to leave the room with him. When they were gone, Paul pulled up a chair and started through the story of how she had been injured, how the two high school kids had been killed, how Griffin and Fenner had done it, and the difficulties of bringing Griffin to justice. As the narrative unfolded, Joan's face reddened, her eyes darkened, and her heart monitor beeped faster. When Paul finished, she remained silent for a few minutes. Her heart monitor calmed down some, but her face remained a picture of anger.

"The last thing I knew a dog and some otters had died," Joan finally said. "My god. Two kids dead. Me almost killed and maybe disabled for life. A perfect storm of retaliation for the fiasco two years ago. Why didn't we see it coming?"

"How could we?" said Paul.

"Maybe we could have found out who Jake's brother is and kept tabs on him or something? Worked harder to find out where Griffin was?"

"Easy to say in retrospect. But not realistic, I think."

"What now?"

"I was afraid you'd ask that. Joan, I won't be around for a couple of days. You're doing well and are in good hands."

"Oh god, Paul. Please tell me you're not going to go off half-cocked like two years ago and do something stupid. I need you."

"Joanie, I couldn't be more in control." Paul wasn't as sure of that as he tried to make it sound. "And I will be fine and I will be back. Count on it."

"Well I know there's nothing I can do to keep you here. Does anyone know what your plans are?"

"No one but me."

"Take care, tough guy."

Paul rose from the chair, bent to embrace Joan, and was pleased at the strength of the hug she was able to give him. "Love you babe," he said, and he left the room.

CHAPTER 41

Before leaving Traverse City, Paul stopped at his bank and withdrew five thousand dollars in cash. He didn't know how much he would actually need, but he figured that where he was going there would be times when he would not want to use his credit card, or it might be refused even if he did. He then drove the fifteen miles north to Elk Rapids in the late afternoon sun, glad to be heading back to his boat if only for one night. Elk Rapids was charming as ever as he drove slowly along River Street in the lazy sparse traffic. He envied the residents and tourists who strolled along the sidewalks past the geranium pots and maple saplings with seemingly not a care in the world. He stopped to pick up some take-out dinner, drove down into the marina lot, locked the Mustang and went to his boat. *Tondeleyo* seemed a little neglected and forlorn, perhaps mostly in Paul's imagination.

Paul unlocked the main hatch and threw his sea bag down into the salon. He got the water hose from the dock service pedestal and washed down the deck and cabin tops. Going below he found that the sun had warmed up the interior uncomfortably, and he opened all of the ventilation hatches, hoping not to have to turn on the air conditioner. He pulled a cold beer out of the fridge and went back up into the cockpit. Few people were around in the marina, but those who were there had the same air of contentment and lack of worldly problems as did the pedestrians up on River Street.

The seagulls went about their business peacefully too. But the beauty of the placid harbor was lost on him.

He finished his beer and went below to pack for tomorrow's trip. He pulled out an old water-resistant backpack from one of the seat lockers and loaded it with a small collection of clothing—one spare lightweight polo shirt, one spare pair of pants, one pair of shorts, some underwear, a foul-weather windbreaker, and his dopp kit. He threw in a couple of paperback books for the airports between flights. He ate the burger and salad from River Street with another beer, and went back topside. He had two phone calls to make.

He dialed his dad in Chicago and brought him up to date on all that had happened since they had been together in Chicago.

"Jesus Christ Paul, that's unbelievable," said Brian Tyson. "I'm so sorry about all of it. We knew Griffin was a son of a bitch, but killing people? Thank god Joan is coming around. So what's next?"

"I'm taking a little trip."

"Care to elaborate?"

"Not right now Dad. You'll have to trust me on this one."

"I've long since quit trying to ride herd on you, Fireball. You know you have my trust. Just be careful. Any way I can help? Money?"

"I'm good." Paul's dad was loaded, but Paul did not like to rely on that if he didn't have to.

"Okay. Go for it."

"See you, dad."

Paul prepared to dial Craig Basham. This was the conversation Paul dreaded most. Craig would have a pretty good idea of what Paul was up to and would not approve in the least.

"Craig, it's Paul."

"What's up?"

"I'll be AWOL for a few days."

"What? Oh no you don't."

"Got to Craig."

"Can you talk about it?"

"I don't want you to be able to talk about it or lie about it. I want you to be able to say you don't know where I am. And in general that will be true. Because I don't know either, for sure."

"Is there anything I can do to talk you out of it?"

"Not a fucking thing, dude."

"Thought so. Be careful hotshot."

They ended the call, and Paul went below to do some computer work. He pulled up the Internet and got a Google map of the Virgin Islands. He thought about a way to get to Isla Colombo from St. Thomas that did not involve a passport check on the island. Then he focused on a detailed map and satellite view of Isla Colombo itself, got oriented as to where the med school was, and where the various bays were in relation to the school and the town of Cristobal. He printed out some images to take with him on the plane flights. Finally, he registered on line for a tour of the med school for prospective students three days from now. He shut down the computer and read for a while before going to bed early. He had to get up at 4:30 a.m.

CHAPTER 42

Paul was deeply asleep at 4:30 a.m. when his alarm clock jangled him awake. Wide-eyed instantly, he rose quickly and dressed in a maroon polo shirt, tan cargo shorts, boat shoes and a plain khaki ball cap. He specifically avoided wearing any of his usual tee shirts and ball caps with the "RULI" institute logo. He drank a quick glass of orange juice, grabbed his backpack, locked up the boat and went up to his car. Twenty-five minutes later he was going through the security line at the Traverse City airport munching on a fast food breakfast sandwich.

The 6:00 a.m. flight got him to Detroit Metro in barely enough time for his connecting flight to Atlanta. He had to jog through the long tunnel from Concourse C to Concourse A, trying his best to ignore the hideous neon light show along the walls. Paul was the last to board the loaded plane, but then was able to relax a bit for the two-hour flight to Atlanta. In Atlanta he had a more comfortable hour and a half layover, but still had to walk what seemed like a mile to the gate for the St. Thomas flight. The gate area was not crowded this time of year like it would be in winter time. Sitting impatiently and watching the clock, Paul was tempted to call Joan, but he didn't want to have to dance around what his plans were, and wanted her to concentrate on getting better. And he didn't really have much of a plan other than getting into Griffin's med school and somehow finding out whatever he could. He got a sandwich for lunch instead.

The flight to St. Thomas droned on through the afternoon, with spectacular views of the deep blue ocean and the sun-bathed islands of the Bahamas and the Eastern Caribbean. In the late afternoon Paul could see Puerto Rico below his window as the plane began its final approach to St. Thomas just to the east. The smooth landing brought back memories of his visit to St. Thomas with his parents when he was a teenager twenty years ago. At Cyril King airport there are no jetways for deplaning, just the old fashioned mobile stairways, and at the open door of the plane Paul was hit hard by the humid 90 degrees.

After clearing customs and immigration in the airport it was nearly dusk when Paul got to the rental car desks and rented a Ford Focus. It would be dark soon and Paul did not want to attempt the drive through rush hour traffic in Charlotte Amalie and over to the east side of the island, especially having to drive on the left side and not knowing the roads all that well. So after leaving the airport he stopped at the first small hotel he came to and got a room for the night. More fast food nearby for dinner, and then early to bed.

CHAPTER 43

After breakfast the next morning, Paul drove on through Charlotte Amalie on Veterans Drive along the waterfront. It was already getting hot. The white and pastel buildings and houses, tightly stacked all the way up the hills to the left, were ablaze in sunlight, and the wide bay to the right sparkled riotously. There was only one cruise ship over at the long concrete pier; in winter there would be four or five on many days. Paul was nervous driving on the left side, and he drew several angry honks at a tricky intersection on the east side of town where he needed to get over onto Route 38. After that it was pretty smooth going as he drove eastward for a number of miles and turned onto Route 32 that led the rest of the way to the eastern tip of the island. At 9:30 a.m. he arrived in Red Hook, the small port town on Vessup Bay at the mouth of Red Hook Bay.

Paul parked in one of the lots along the shopping strip in Red Hook. He walked across the street and over to the ferry dock. He inquired about a ticket to Isla Colombo, but was told that Americans now needed a special visa, and those were hard to come by these days. Paul assumed that he would have the same problem with air service to Isla Colombo, and he went to plan B. He walked back along the waterfront to the marina. There were several boats with signs advertising their availability for fishing charters; Paul figured a fishing yacht would not be too conspicuous hanging around

Isla Colombo. He spoke to the captain of the first charter boat he came to.

"Can you take me fishing to Isla Colombo?"

"Why there?"

"I've been to most of the islands, but not that one, and I hear the fishing's great there."

"Well you heard wrong, and I won't go there anyway."

"Why not?"

"American flagged boats are not welcome there. Politics."

Paul wasn't surprised to hear this. He went to the next charter boat, and he got the same response. And he got the same response from all of the other charter captains in the marina. He left the marina and drove a half mile or so over to Saphire Beach and tried the marina there. Again there were several charter boats, but none would take him to Isla Colombo.

"Shit," said Paul at the last one.

"Try the marina over on Benner Bay," said the fishing captain. "It's back along Red Hook Road a few miles. Might be some dude there who would take you."

"Thanks," said Paul.

Paul backtracked along Red Hook Road, which was the local name for Route 32. The marina was right next to the road on Benner Bay, which faced southward. It was hotter now and the sun was relentless. Paul parked the Ford and prowled the docks until he found the oldest, seediest charter boat in the marina. He had gotten the message at the other more upscale marinas that he would get nowhere with the newer, fancier boats. This one was an old 40-foot Hatteras, a dirty white flybridge fishing cruiser with harbor oil smudge all around the water line. In the cockpit fighting chair sat a wreck of a man who was probably 50 but looked 65. His bleached and graying hair was loosely pulled back in a pony tail, and he wore only a pair of torn cut-off jeans and flip flops. He was deep-tanned brown and wrinkled, and he was a few teeth shy of needing dentures. He and his boat looked like they had not had much business lately. Paul thought he might get lucky here, if this damn tub could make it to Isla Colombo and back.

"Hey cap," said Paul cheerfully.

"'Sup buddy?" rasped the man through a tobacco-ravaged voice box.

"I'm looking for a charter over to the Isla Colombo waters."

"No can do, Kemosabee. Bad karma over there."

"Look cap, you don't look so damn busy. I can pay good. What the hell?"

The man spat, barely clearing the transom, and stroked his chin stubble. After a long several minutes, he replied.

"Five hundred bucks a day, plus you buy the fuel and provisions."

"Jesus Christ. Well, okay. Can we leave first thing in the morning?"

"Yep, if I can get my mate outta the sack and get some things shipshape. ANNIE, GET YOUR ASS UP HERE. WE GOT A JOB."

A scrawny girl of no more than sixteen appeared at the cockpit door and squinted in the sunlight. Her faded yellow bikini was skimpy but it didn't have much to cover. She reached up and tried to tidy up her thatch of brown hair that hadn't seen a comb in days.

"Clean up the galley and check all the fishing gear," ordered the captain. "This is first mate Annie," he said to Paul. "My name is Kirk."

"Kirk the Jerk," said Annie.

"Shut up, squirt," grinned Kirk.

Paul puzzled at what the hell sort of relationship this was, but gave up. *Whatever. Captain Kirk, eh? Well this sure ain't the Starship Enterprise.* He addressed Captain Kirk. "My name is Paul Tyson. So where do I get the provisions?"

"There's a grocery store across the road and down a ways, can't miss it. How many days we talking about?"

"Two, maybe three," replied Paul.

"Okay. Get whatever you like, but bring lots of beer."

"Okay. Your fridge works, right?"

"Of course."

"By the way, do you carry snorkel gear?"

"Yeah, we got some."

Paul went back along the rickety dock to his car, wondering what he was getting himself into here, but remained determined to get over to Isla Colombo. He drove the short distance to the grocery store and filled a shopping cart with eggs, bread, lunch meat, a bunch of canned goods and two cases of Carib beer. He returned the stuff to the boat, and said he would be back later after returning his rental car.

"We'll be right here," said the captain.

Chapter 44

Paul was able to return the car nearby at Saphire beach, where his rental company had a branch office. On the way through Red Hook, he stopped at the fancy marina store and bought a British yacht flag, thinking they might need that as a cover over at Isla Colombo. The British Virgins were just to the east of St. Thomas, and lots of yachts operated there.

He parked the car at the Saphire beach office and took a walk out onto the beach in front of the condo complex where he and his parents had stayed twenty years ago. The sun-dappled blue water was as clear and beautiful as he remembered it. He daydreamed a while thinking of all the great snorkeling beaches here on the east end, including Secret Harbor, Cowpet Bay, Lindquist Beach, and his favorite, Cokie Beach. The water was clearest at Cokie and the swarms of incredible fish were breathtaking. The nearby Coral World people fed the fish regularly, and the fish tamely nibbled at your fingers and toes looking for more. Paul could see part of St. John over to the south, and he remembered the beautiful beaches they visited there too.

Paul got a ride from the rental company back to the marina and returned to the boat, which was named Pirate's Pleasure. *Wonderful. Didn't notice that earlier.* Her engine was running, and Kirk and Annie were tying her up after a visit to the gas dock. At least the engines sounded pretty good. As Paul got aboard, Kirk handed him the receipt for the gas. Paul looked at it and blinked at the figure: thirteen hundred and change.

"Good god."

"Tanks weren't even empty either, dude. Now for the charter fee, I want seven fifty up front." Paul pulled out his wallet and started counting out hundred dollar bills.

Paul stowed his backpack in the small stateroom that Annie said he could use, located below and forward on the starboard side of a hallway leading to the owner's stateroom at the bow. He spent the afternoon wandering around the marina, and had an early dinner at a small ramshackle restaurant nestled against the harborside mangrove trees. The pulled-pork sandwich and cold beer were delicious in the slight breeze on the canopy-covered verandah.

Back aboard *Pirate's Pleasure,* Paul read one of his paperback books in his bunk before drifting off to sleep in the welcome cool air of the air-conditioner; fortunately the AC worked well.

Chapter 45

In the morning Paul was awakened by the clang of pots and pans up in the galley, and he looked at his watch. *Jesus Christ, it's nine thirty already.* He had a two p.m. appointment for the tour of the med school. He got into his tan shorts and a white tee shirt and went up to where the racket was. Annie was scrambling some eggs.

"Want some coffee?" she said.

"Absolutely," Paul replied. "Where's the boss? We gotta get going."

"Kirk the Jerk? Still asleep. I'll get him up soon."

"You get away with that 'Jerk' stuff?"

"Oh yeah. He's a pussy cat. Pirate my ass!"

"If you say so. Good coffee."

"Thanks. You can make some toast over there."

"Gotcha." Paul made toast and filled a plate with eggs from the pan.

The captain eventually came coughing and spitting up into the galley, grunted a greeting and grabbed some coffee. He took the coffee out to the cockpit and up to the flybridge, where he started the diesel engines to warm them up. Back down in the main cabin the captain spread out a chart on the navigation table and looked at Isla Colombo. He looked up the GPS coordinates and entered them in the chart plotter. "ETD fifteen minutes," he barked into the galley. He was communicating the estimated time of departure. Paul thought maybe this guy would be okay after all.

Paul went on deck with Annie, who was still in her little bikini. They unhooked and stowed the electric cables and the water hose, and stood by to take in the mooring lines. Captain Kirk went back up on the flybridge and said, "Let's go." Paul threw the bow line aboard, Annie did the stern line and then the two spring lines, and they stepped aboard. Kirk backed the boat away from the dock and headed slowly southward out of the marina, the engine rumbling softly.

Clearing the channel out into Jersey Bay, Kirk throttled up to ten miles per hour and headed due east to get past the shoals along the south side of the bay. On the left Paul could see Secret Harbor in Nazareth Bay where he and his parents had snorkeled. It was peaceful with several sailboats basking in the sun at anchor offshore. Kirk then turned southeast, kicked her up to 22 mph, and roared out of Jersey Bay with the stern firmly squatted in the huge wake.

Paul joined Kirk on the flybridge, his hair flying in the brisk southeast breeze. *Pirate's Pleasure* was taking the three-foot waves in stride as they passed by Little James Island with St. John looming further off to port, and the open sea was dazzling in the rising sunlight. Paul would rather have been sailing, but that would have been impractical for this mission. Annie was down in the cockpit getting fishing equipment ready, but Paul refrained from telling her that there actually would not be any fishing on this trip. He didn't want Kirk to know that, at least not until they got over to Isla Colombo and Paul could get ashore for what he needed to do.

Southeast was about the perfect course for the run to Isla Colombo, which sat to the south of the British Virgins at the eastern angle of an imaginary equilateral triangle with St. Thomas and St. Croix at the two other angles to the west. At 22 mph it would take less than two hours to get to Isla Colombo. Paul went below to look at the maps he had downloaded back at home, to refresh his memory of the location he had chosen to attempt his invasion of the island.

He brought his paperback book up to the cockpit and relaxed on a padded bench for the rest of the run. Annie finished with the fishing gear and went into the galley to make some sandwiches for lunch.

At noon Kirk called down from the flybridge, "We're approaching the island, Tyson."

Paul went up and sat beside the captain. He squinted at the chart plotter screen, which showed an image of a nautical chart overlayed with a radar image and their GPS position which was displayed on the chart. He looked for the bay in which the harbor of the town of Cristobal was located, and then found the next bay to the north.

"Can you go into Stingray Bay there?"

"What for," asked Kirk.

"I want to snorkel in there. I hear it's great."

"I thought this was a fishing charter."

"Later."

"I don't want to get too close."

"Just give it a try, please. I have a British flag you can fly, if that would help."

"Okay. Give it to Annie."

Paul went below and got the flag from his backpack, and Annie clipped it to the jackstaff. When they got partway into the bay, Paul pressed his luck with Kirk a little more.

"Can you anchor?"

"Absolutely not. I would technically have landed illegally on the island, and could get arrested, lose my boat, and sit in jail forever."

"Well, can Annie row me ashore in your inflatable while you stand offshore out here?"

"What the hell are you up to, Tyson. I don't like the trend of this."

"Okay. Here's the thing. My girlfriend is a student at the med school here. I want to sneak over there and surprise her with a couple days' fishing trip."

"You're nuts dude."

"I'll pay extra. I'm counting on this, cap."

Kirk thought for a while. "Another five hundred. Now."

"You got it." Paul pulled some more bills from his wallet, and went to get Annie to set up the inflatable dingy. Then he went below to change from his tee shirt to a blue polo shirt, and put on his boat shoes. He pocketed his smartphone, not because he expected to make any calls but because it could take pictures. He left his passport in the backpack, as it would be useless here.

After eating the sandwiches, Paul and Annie deployed the dingy, and Annie started rowing for shore.

"I should be back by five p.m.," shouted Paul to Kirk.

"You better be, or we'll be gone."

Paul waved and faced toward shore. Annie rowed surprisingly strongly. There were no other boats in the bay; it was not cruising season. When they got close to shore, Annie said he would have to get out now; she was warned by Kirk not to touch land. Paul took off his boat shoes and carried them as he got out and waded ashore. He walked up the beach and through some sea grape to the road. He sat down and brushed the sand off of his feet, put on his boat shoes, and started walking south toward town.

Chapter 46

Walking toward town in the baking sun, Paul began to seriously doubt the wisdom of this escapade he had rashly rushed into. His only real plan was to get inside the med school. What specifically to do there and how to get away with it and get safely back off this rather unattractive island had never been worked out in his mind. But despair over Joan's condition and anger at Larry Griffin drove him onward. After walking three quarters of a mile, Paul was in the outskirts of the town of Cristobal and came upon the motor scooter rental place he had located from his Google search back at home.

Isla Colombo Motors had a scooter available for him, and thankfully they did not ask for any ID; they surely would have questioned how an American got on the island, and maybe reported it to the police. Paul paid cash, one hundred dollars for the afternoon; dollars are accepted virtually throughout the Caribbean island nations regardless of politics. He consulted his map and started off, glad to be driving on the right side of the road again. The main street of the small town led directly to the road over to the med school, and he headed east out into the flat, dry interior of the island, passing lots of scrub vegetation and low-lying cactus. The heat radiated off of the straight two-lane blacktop and blasted Paul in the face as the scooter whined along at forty mph.

Ten minutes later Paul approached the med school, a cluster of pink stucco buildings that had little in the way of style. No traditional Spanish architecture here. He could see and hear the Atlantic Ocean behind them. He stopped at the security gate at the entrance and said he had an appointment for the prospective student tour. The guard looked for Paul's name in the day's roster sheet and found it, waving him through. He parked near the front of the administration building and walked into the front office. The receptionist found Paul's name in the list.

"What is your nationality, Mr. Tyson?"

Paul blinked for a beat. "Canadian." Americans who are abroad and want to avoid anti-Americanism frequently claim to be Canadian. Paul was again relieved not to have to show his ID. Apparently this school was hungry for students and was not fussy about the current state of politics over in Cristobal.

"Excellent. We have several Canadian students here. Please join the tour group in the next room on the right down the hall."

"Thank you, miss."

"De nada, señior," said the young lady with a warm smile.

Paul entered the waiting room and sat down among nine other men and women of various ages; many students at these island med schools were redirecting their career paths, including PhDs in the life sciences who were attracted by an accelerated MD program. Fifteen minutes later a middle-aged woman entered the room wearing a lab coat with a badge that had an MD next to her name. She welcomed the group and outlined the plan for the afternoon's tour. After showing an overview video on a large flat-screen wall monitor, she led them out of the building and over to the first of several buildings that were on the schedule. After touring the gross anatomy lab, where a number of cadavers lay on gurneys in various states of dissection, the group was shown several research labs.

Paul finally found paydirt when the guide said, "This next lab is that of the renowned Dr. Manuel Mendoza, who is doing cutting-edge work in medical gene technology and is close to developing cures for several major genetic diseases." Paul had heard many claims like this before and was skeptical, but no matter. This was where Griffin was doing his dirty work. Paul hung to the rear of the group in case Griffin was in the lab, but no one seemed to be there. The group entered briefly, and Paul saw the seawater tanks with the small jellyfish drifting around in them. His blood pressure skyrocketed, and he hoped no one saw the beet-red color that flushed into his face. He could no longer hear the guide over the pounding pulse in his ears. He calmed down some as the group was led out and down the hall to the next destination. Paul got himself into the middle of the group to try to avoid being seen by Griffin if he happened to pass by.

A few minutes later on the second floor the group was shown one of the lecture arenas, where a lecture was in session. Paul was pleased to see that Griffin was sitting in the back row, slouching and not paying much attention. Griffin glanced over at the group, but Paul had anticipated that and had stepped behind one of the taller tour members. The tour group left, and as it rounded a corner Paul hung back and turned back down the hallway. He quickly went back downstairs and down the hall to the Mendoza lab. It still appeared to be empty. *Not much security around here*, Paul thought. *Good thing for me.* Paul quietly approached the jellyfish tanks, pulled out his smartphone, and began taking a video of them. Griffin's name was written on a strip of white tape affixed to all three of them. After panning the camera around the lab, he stepped to a nearby desk and found papers and lab books with Griffin's name on them. He found one labeled "Freshwater Jellyfish Transgenics" and photographed the cover and several pages of notes.

Paul figured he was running out of time, and started to leave. But his anger got the best of him. He picked up a heavy magnetic stirring machine and hurled it at one of the jellyfish tanks. The glass shattered and the water cascaded to the floor. Paul stepped back, grabbed two more heavy objects and threw them at the other two tanks, which burst and disgorged their contents. A door at the rear of the lab banged open, and Dr. Mendoza, who had just returned from Cuba that morning, rushed into the lab with his mouth agape.

"QUE PASA? WHAT THE HELL ARE YOU DOING? WHO ARE YOU?"

Paul ran out of the lab and out of the building toward the parking lot in front of the administration building. He jumped on the rental scooter and gunned it toward the entrance gate. The guard had a cell phone at his ear and was trying to get the gate closed as Paul roared past him and down the road back to Cristobal. He was only halfway to town when he saw two police cars coming toward him. They stopped, blocking the road, and Paul slowed to a stop in front of them. *Oh boy.*

At 5 p.m. Captain Kirk took one more look at the shore with his binoculars from his position out at the mouth of the Stingray Bay. "No sign of him. We're outta here." He gunned the engines, spun the wheel, and roared off to the northwest.

CHAPTER 47

Paul sat on the padded bench of his jail cell with his head in his hands. *Jesus Christ. Back in jail again 'cause of my goddamn temper.* He was painfully remembering his arrest two years ago for the alleged assault of Ron Withers, whom Paul had publically threatened for plagiarizing his dissertation data. Though innocent, Paul had spent two days in jail and several weeks under indictment, eventually for murder when Withers died of his accidental injury, before being acquitted at trial. But Paul was not innocent this time, nor did he have access to decent legal representation.

Paul's cell was at the end of a row of five cells in the male section of the jailhouse. The cells were separated by steel vertical bars, and Paul had seen that all of the other cells were empty except for one in the middle of the row, where a native islander was sleeping on his bench. After a while Paul lay down on his bench with one arm across his face to shield his eyes from the glare of the ceiling lights.

The jail guard sat at a desk in a small vestibule between the male and female sections of the jail. He was reading a porno magazine as a man approached him from the outer entrance of the jailhouse. That man was Larry Griffin.

"Si?" said the guard.

Griffin peered around the corners into the two sections to locate Paul Tyson, and was pleased to find that there was another prisoner in that section. He quietly spoke to the

Guard. "Habla Englés?" Griffin had some Spanish but preferred not to have to struggle with it.

"Si."

Griffin showed the guard a mailing envelope and pulled a cell phone out of it. "I brought a cell phone for my cousin. His mother, my aunt, is dying and the family wants him to speak with her."

"Not allowed, señior."

"Would this help?" Griffin pulled a hundred dollars' worth of peso notes out of his pocket.

"Maybe." The guard reached for the mailing envelope and felt it to see if any sort of weapon was in it. No weapon. The guard took the money, gestured for Griffin to go ahead, and resumed his perusal of the magazine.

Griffin stopped at the middle cell, slid the envelope under the bars toward the sleeping prisoner, and proceeded down to Paul's cell.

"Well, hot shot. Things are not going so hot now, are they?"

Pulling his elbow away from his eyes, Paul looked over at Griffin and then rose from the bench and stalked over to the door of his cell. Grabbing the bars violently, he searched for words. Finally he spat out, "You son of a bitch, we've got you."

"Oh you do? Looks like it's the other way around. You're in here for entering the country illegally and malicious destruction of property. You're going to rot in here for a very long time. They don't take kindly to Americans who do what you did."

"How did *you* get in to the country, asshole?" said Paul.

"They make an exception for students at the med school. You only need a pulse for that. How is Joan?"

"Just fine."

"I'll bet. I heard otherwise. Anyway, thanks for conveniently destroying the evidence in my lab."

"There are notebooks…"

"They will burn just fine dude."

Paul did not bother to say that he had photos, because the police had taken his smartphone. All he could say was, "Fenner will finger you."

"They don't extradite Americans here, and there's lots of other places in the world I can be a rich doctor."

"Some humanitarian you are. How did you get to be such a vicious son of a bitch? Your mama take away your teddy bear too soon or something?"

Griffin reached through and grabbed Paul's shirt and pulled him up hard against the bars. "Just leave my mother out of this, goddamn you," Griffin seethed. He shoved Paul halfway back across the cell room and stalked back up the hallway.

Out in his car on the way back to the med school, Griffin finally failed to avoid remembering the last time he saw his mother. His memory insisted on replaying the scene: it was the day after he had graduated from high school. He was in his room at home when his mother came to the door in a thin negligee. She weaved across the room to him and told him how sexy he looked. She pushed herself against him and tried to kiss him, reeking of alcohol. He was trying to tell her not to do this when his father appeared at the door, apparently home early from work and apparently drunk too. His dad roared, "What the fuck are you doing, you whoring bitch?" and came over and pulled her to the floor by the hair. Griffin threw a haymaker punch that landed square in his dad's face and knocked him to the floor. He kicked his dad in the side of the head and walked out of the house, never to return.

In the jail the sleeping prisoner had been awakened by the talking, and he noticed the mailing envelope on the floor near him. He opened it and found the cell phone along with fifty dollars worth of pesos and a handwritten note. The note was in Spanish, and it said *Watch the gringo in the end cell, and if he does anything unusual, or is taken away, call me at the number at the bottom of the page. Speak in Spanish and say "Grandma how are you?" Then very quietly tell me what is happening, in English if you can, or Spanish if necessary. There will be more money if you do this.* The prisoner looked over at Paul, shrugged, and put the phone in his pocket. Paul was already back on his bench lying down.

After what seemed like hours, Paul wondered what time it was. They had taken his watch along with his wallet and phone. Not his belt though. *Guess they don't care if I hang myself. Probably hope I do.*

Shortly an old man came down the hall pushing a cart with two trays on it. He shoved one under the door of the other prisoner's cell and one under Paul's. It contained a metal dish of rice and beans, a slice of bread, and a cup of water. Paul pointed to his wrist and raised his eyebrows in question, and the man showed him his watch. Eight p.m. The man shuffled off.

Paul consumed all of his food and water, used the toilet in the corner of the cell, and settled back on his bench for what he figured would be a long night.

Chapter 48

At 9 a.m. the next morning, the Cristobal jailhouse guard was just starting a new issue of a porno magazine when a young woman in a nurse's uniform approached him. It was Juanita Salazar. She was carrying a small medical kit and a tall cardboard cup of Starbucks coffee. "Hola, Raoul." Juanita knew the guard from high school days.

"Juanita! I have not seen your lovely face for ages. What are you doing here?"

"I am bringing you this coffee, and a medical kit to examine your prisoner Mr. Tyson."

"Tyson? Why?"

"Yesterday he was touring the medical school where I work, and they had a form he had filled out that stated that he is a diabetic. I have been told to check his blood sugar and give him insulin if he needs it."

"Hmmm. I would think they would prefer that he die of the disease. Whatever. Go ahead. He is in the cell down at the end of that hallway. Can you do it through the bars, or do I have to let you in?"

"I can do it through the bars. Thank you Raoul," she replied with as sexy a smile as she could muster. She rounded the corner into the male section and walked to the end cell.

"Mr. Tyson?"

Paul sat up on the bench and stared at the beautiful nurse standing at the bars of his cell door.

"Mr. Tyson, I am here to check on your diabetes condition."

"What? I don't..."

"Shhh," said Juanita quietly with her finger to her lips. She looked over at the other prisoner and saw that he was watching her. She motioned with her hand for Paul to come to her, and spoke softly and quickly.

"I am from the med school. I made up the diabetes story, but I have to pretend to test you and treat you. I know what you were doing at the school and I want to help you."

"But who are you and why..."

"Be quiet and give me your finger for the blood glucose test." As she pricked his finger and dabbed at the blood with the tester she explained. "I am Juanita Salazar. I know that Larry Griffin has killed and injured people in Michigan with his horrible creation, and I want him to be caught and prosecuted, hopefully with a death penalty. If I can help you, maybe there will be a better chance of that."

"You seem to have more of a motive than that," said Paul, seeing the hatred in her eyes.

"He has treated me very badly. I hate him deeply. Now let me pretend to give you an insulin shot. Turn your arm to the bars." As she proceeded with the sham, she continued to speak, now in a whisper.

"I will return tomorrow morning to do this again, but I will disable the guard and get you out of here. You must be prepared to run with me."

"How are you..."

"Shhh. It will work. Now adios until tomorrow."

Paul watched her in amazement as she walked back up the hall.

In the middle cell, the prisoner pulled out the cell phone and dialed the number on the note from the envelope. "Hola Abuela. Cómo te sientes hoy?" he said, and then more softly, "A pretty nurse came and did some kind of treatment to the gringo, and talked for a while, then left."

"Call me immediately if she comes again," replied Griffin. "You will be paid well."

Juanita stopped beside the guard, gave him a big smile, and put her hand on his arm. Squeezing it gently, she said "Thank you again, handsome!"

"Thank you for the coffee, mi corazón. I hope I see you again!"

"I will be here every day."

Raoul watched her lovely backside as she walked away toward the main entrance. She added a bit of extra sway in her hips for his benefit, knowing that for some reason men everywhere found nurses' uniforms to be sexy, and she wanted to heighten his interest for her return tomorrow. Raoul turned back to his porno magazine with a very red face.

Juanita drove the short distance to the marina and went to her brother's boat.

"Luis, you must help me, and there is much to do today. Our lives are going to change in a very big way, and forever."

"Anything for you, Juanita. What will we do?"

Juanita began to describe her plan.

Chapter 49

Later that same morning up in Traverse City, Joan Brockton lay in her hospital bed exhausted from her session with the physical therapists. They had worked her arms and upper torso mercilessly, and had her wiggling her toes with all her might. She was starting to be able to move her feet, and they made her repeat that until she ran out of steam.

"We'll be back tomorrow," said one of the therapists.

"I was afraid of that," replied Joan.

Joan was still breathing hard when Craig Basham knocked and entered her room.

"Hi Joan. How goes it?"

"They're trying to kill me."

"Who is?" said Craig, looking startled.

"Those therapists."

"Oh. Yeah. They can be brutal. But they'll get you better sooner."

"I know, I know. What's happening? Do you know anything about Paul?"

"Nothing about Paul. But I have learned that Jerry Fenner has made a plea bargain. After his indictment yesterday, he got a reduced charge in turn for describing Griffin's actions and agreeing to testify against him."

"Well, that's something anyway, if they can ever get at Griffin. But I'm worried as hell about Paul. You know his hot head as well as I do."

"I do indeed, and I worry too. All we can do is wait and wonder. But let's concentrate on getting you better."

"Yep. Thanks Craig."

Craig left the room and greeted the Brocktons, who were coming down the hall.

CHAPTER 50

The next morning Paul ravenously ate his breakfast of beans and rice and awaited the arrival of the nurse, Juanita. He had no idea what she had in store for him, and doubted that it would work, whatever it was. But he could hardly get into worse trouble than he already was in, unless he were to be involved in assaulting or killing someone. *God, I hope she doesn't have that in mind.*

At 9:30 a.m. Juanita came into the jailhouse, again carrying the medical kit and a tall cup of coffee. Raoul looked up from his desk and grinned broadly as she approached him.

"Hola, handsome!" she said. "More coffee, a latte supreme today."

"Gracias, my sweet."

She turned and perched one side of her behind on his desk inches from his right hand, and he brushed it against that luscious curve bulging beneath the white dress as he reached for the coffee. He took three big gulps as he tried to steady himself from the wave of lust that was making him dizzy.

"How are you today Raoul?" she said.

"Excellent," he said, drinking some more of the coffee. "I would be even better if we could get together tonight after work."

"I would love that," replied Juanita. "Enjoy your coffee while I tend to the prisoner, and then we can make plans. By the way, where do you keep the personal effects of the prisoners, in case he has any medicines that he needs?"

"In that drawer there." He pointed to a double file cabinet beside his desk, where there was a drawer with a piece of tape labeled *Tyson*. "But he had no medicines."

"Okay. See you in a few minutes."

Juanita went down to Paul's cell and began repeating the medical charade with Paul, hoping she had calculated the right amount of Nembutal to put in the coffee such that Raoul would soon lose consciousness for a while but would not die.

The other prisoner immediately dialed his cell phone, repeated the grandma greeting, and said "She is here." He put away the phone.

Juanita whispered, "The guard should fall asleep soon, and then I will get his keys and get you out of here. We will get your things from the cabinet next to him, and run to my car which is parked across the street."

"Then what?" asked Paul.

"We go to Stingray Beach, swim to my brother's boat, and go to St. Thomas."

"But this is so risky for both of you. How can you do this?"

"I have made up my mind to do this, and my brother will do anything to help me."

There was a clatter as the guard's chair fell over and the coffee splashed on the floor. Juanita quickly walked up the hall and found Raoul on the floor. She shook him, but found that he was thoroughly unconscious. *Don't die, please.* She opened the drawer of his desk, grabbed a ring of keys, and ran back to Paul's cell. The third key she tried opened his door. They ran up the hall and stepped around the guard to the file cabinet. In the Tyson drawer were Paul's wallet and watch. His smartphone was not there. All of Paul's cash was missing from his wallet, but his ID and credit cards were still there. They ran through the empty main hallway, out the front entrance, and across the street to her car. She pulled away from the curb and headed straight ahead down the road toward Stingray Beach.

As Juanita's car passed the first intersection, which was the main street that led over to the med school, Larry Griffin was coming fast in his car on that street on his way to the jail. Recognizing her car and seeing Paul in the passenger seat, Griffin turned the corner and followed her. He hung back a little so as not to give himself away just yet.

Juanita stopped the car on the shoulder alongside Stingray Bay, and she and Paul jumped out and ran down across the beach.

"That is Luis out there!" shouted Juanita as she waved at the boat idling in the middle of the bay. "He doesn't have a dingy, and we have to swim."

They stopped at the water's edge and kicked off their shoes, and Juanita tore off her nurse's dress. She had a swimsuit underneath. Unaware that Larry Griffin had arrived and was now running toward the beach, they strode into the calm water and began swimming.

Halfway out to Luis's boat, Paul felt something grab one of his feet and drag him backwards. He twisted around and saw Griffin's fist just before it landed on Paul's jaw. Stunned, Paul was unable to get in any kind of a defensive move before Griffin had his arms around Paul's neck and was pulling Paul down underwater. Paul struggled, trying to punch Griffin as best he could, but in the water it was ineffective. Unable to get his head above water, Paul became desperate for air. Choking on water now, Paul knew he was on the way to being drowned. He was trying to reach for Griffin's vulnerable crotch when his face suddenly started burning as though it were in boiling water. Griffin's grasp loosened, and Paul managed to pull to the surface. Griffin was gasping and grabbing at his own face.

Juanita had kept on swimming, initially unaware of the fight. When she finally heard the commotion she looked back and saw the splashing and struggling. She swam back toward Paul and his attacker, whom she knew must be Larry Griffin. Griffin turned back toward shore, and Paul shouted to Juanita.

"JELLYFISH! BE CAREFUL."

Juanita kept on swimming until she got near Paul.

"Are you alright?" she shouted.

"I think so," replied Paul, coughing. "Just hurts like hell."

She turned and screamed at the boat. "LUIS, HELP US."

Luis had been in the cabin looking at charts and listening on the radio for any talk of a jail escape in town. He rushed out onto the fantail, and Juanita shouted again.

"PAUL NEEDS VINEGAR FOR JELLYFISH STINGS" She turned back to Paul. "Swim to the boat and Luis will put some vinegar on you."

Luis saw what was happening and immediately knew that Larry Griffin had come. Fearing for Juanita, he quickly pulled out his container of vinegar from a seat locker and set it on the seat. He checked to see that his rigging knife was in its leather case on his belt, kicked off his boat shoes, dove into the water and began swimming toward Juanita. When he got to Paul he told him the vinegar was on the cockpit seat, and resumed swimming toward Juanita.

Juanita saw Griffin stagger in the shallow water toward the beach. He was gasping for air and trying to reach into his pocket. She knew what he was trying to do, and swam toward him. Luis shouted for her to come to the boat, but she ignored him. When she got near Griffin she saw him feebly pull out an EpiPen epinephrine auto-injector. He was going into anaphylactic shock, and she knew that he would probably die without the injection. He fumbled the device and it fell to the sand. Juanita ran up to Griffin and picked up the EpiPen. Griffin tried to speak, but his tongue had swollen to the size of a mango and his airways were rapidly constricting. She thought he was probably saying, "Help me Juanita."

With tears welling out of her eyes, she backed away from Griffin, crossed herself, and then threw the EpiPen as far as she could out into the bay. She looked back at Griffin as he collapsed on the beach and started turning blue. She turned to see Luis coming out of the water with his knife in his hand.

"Put that away, Luis. He can do nothing now. We must go quickly before the police come."

They ran back into the water and swam toward the boat.

Chapter 51

Juanita and Luis pulled themselves onto the swim platform and climbed over the transom into the cockpit of the boat. Paul was lying on the deck squirting vinegar on his face, which had some angry red welts on it.

"Tend to him, Juanita," said Luis. "I must get us out of here." He sprang up the ladder to the flybridge, rammed the gear levers into forward and pressed the throttles wide open. Juanita steadied herself against the fighting chair until the boat planed off and became stable at cruising speed. Then she went to Paul.

"Are you okay Mr. Tyson?"

"It's Paul, please. I'm pretty good. That vinegar really helps."

On the flybridge Luis checked to make sure the horizon was free of any other boats for the time being, engaged the autopilot, and descended to the cockpit.

"It looks like he only has a couple of short tentacle tracks," said Luis. "There must have been just a few stray tentacles drifting out there; they can stay active for a long time after breaking off from the jellyfish."

"It was enough for Griffin," said Juanita. "He was hypersensitive."

"What will happen to him," asked Paul.

"He is probably already dead. God help me."

"Why do you say that?" said Luis.

"Because I could have saved him by helping with his epinephrine injector. But I did not. He was a pig, but I broke my nurse's vows. I killed him." She broke down sobbing. Luis took her in his arms.

"Do not think that way. He was the killer. The world is rid of a vicious killer."

"That was for God to decide," she said.

"I think He did, Juanita." Luis hugged Juanita once more and went to get some dry clothes before going back up to the flybridge.

Juanita got control of herself and went to Paul.

An hour later, Paul was relaxing relatively comfortably on a padded bench on the flybridge alongside Juanita, and Luis was at helm in the captain's chair. The boat planed easily over the slight swell, and the sun shone brightly on the smooth sea surface. Juanita had gotten dressed in shorts and a tee shirt, and Paul was wearing one of Luis's swimsuits and a pair of his flip flops while his clothes were drying in the cockpit.

Down below, the main cabin and the two small staterooms were jam-packed with all of Juanita's possessions, except for her car which remained abandoned by the road at Stingray Bay. She would not ever return to Isla Colombo, nor would Luis. They were outlaws there now.

"I can't believe the police never came," said Luis.

"The guard would not have alerted them for some time, if ever," said Juanita. "I hope I didn't kill him too."

"Will you ever know?" asked Paul.

"I have a good contact at the med school who will know," she replied.

"What will you both do now?"

"We will apply for permanent residence in St. Thomas. I will look for a nursing job, and Luis will continue to be a fishing charter captain. I still have a few months on my student visa from when I was at the nursing school there, and Luis has a permit to operate in U.S. Virgin Island waters.

Hopefully we can make the transition eventually to U.S. citizenship. What about you, Paul?"

"First of all, the fishing captain who brought me to Isla Colombo still has my backpack with my clothes and my passport, and is probably mad at me. I'm sure he left for home a few hours after I disappeared. Luis, can we go into the marina at Benner Bay?"

"Sure. I've been there many times. In fact that is the best place for my boat right now; it is a not-so-fancy place and they are not very fussy about who comes there. We will be there in about half an hour."

Chapter 52

After they tied up in a vacant slip in the marina, Paul walked over to the *Pirate's Pleasure*. Annie was asleep on a cockpit bench.

"Hey Annie!" said Paul.

Annie woke up and squinted at Paul. "You. What the hell happened?"

"I sort of got waylaid. Long story. Is the skipper around?"

Captain Kirk appeared at the cockpit door. "Well, here's our screwball charter customer. Where were you, and what the hell happened to your face?"

"Long story. I need my backpack."

"I need more money."

"You got twelve hundred and fifty bucks, full fuel tanks, and a bunch of food and beer for one day's work. You don't need shit, Cap."

"I do if you want your stuff."

"Look, give me my stuff and a ride to the car rental at Saphire, and I will come back next winter with company and do a real charter trip. I'm finished with the Isla Colombo monkey business."

"Oh for Christ sake. Okay."

On the way to Saphire Beach Paul explained a little of what he was doing at Isla Colombo, but left out most of the incriminating details. He thanked Kirk for the ride, and went in and rented another Ford Focus for a week. He would be returning to Traverse City today or tomorrow, but he would let Luis and Juanita use it for the rest of the time while they figured out their own transportation arrangements.

Paul drove up Route 32 to the shopping center at the intersection on Route 38 and bought a new cell phone and some new boat shoes with his credit card, and got some cash at an ATM. He drove back down to the Benner Bay marina and joined Juanita and Luis on Luis's boat.

"I've got a new phone. But the one they took had my photos of Griffin's tanks and notebooks."

"I've got those pictures too," said Juanita. "My spy, Carlos the custodian, took them for me."

"Wow. That's good to have, even though no one will be prosecuting Griffin now, assuming he has died. How will we know about that?"

"I already know. While you were gone I called Carlos. News travels fast there. They found him dead on the beach. The guard at the jail finally woke up and called for help. They know Luis and I were involved in helping you escape, and they are investigating Griffin's death. An autopsy should show that he died of anaphylaxis from jellyfish stings, so hopefully we won't be wanted for murder. But they will still want us for helping you. Does the U.S. extradite to Isla Colombo?"

"I doubt it," said Paul, "since Isla Colombo refuses extradition to the U.S. But I'll have to check with my lawyer friend at home. I'm going to make some calls up there right now. Luis, here are your flip flops; I have new shoes now."

Paul went onto the foredeck with his new phone, and dialed it.

"Joanie?"

"Paul? My god. Where are you?"

"St. Thomas. Lately from Isla Colombo. I'm going to make a very long story very short, until I get back. I have solid photographic evidence of Griffin's operation. But the operation is all out of commission, and so is he."

"What do you mean? What did you do to him?"

"I did nothing to him. But he is dead. In a way, a victim of his own game. I'll explain it when I see you. I'm going to try to fly this evening, but it will probably have to be tomorrow, with all the connections I have to make. How are you doing?"

"A little better each day. It seems like the physical therapists are killing me, but it is working. I love you and can't wait to see you."

"Likewise Joanie. I'll call when I know my flight schedule. Hi to your folks."

"Bye Paul."

Paul dialed Craig Basham.

"Craig."

"Paul?" My god. Where are you?"

"That's exactly what Joan said. Like I said to her, St. Thomas, lately from Isla Colombo. I'm going to make a very long story very short, until I get back. I have solid photographic evidence of Griffin's operation. But it is all out of commission, and so is he. Griffin is dead, but not by my hand. But I am wanted for illegal entry and malicious destruction of property, and my two new good friends are wanted for aiding my escape. We need to know if the U.S. extradites to Isla Colombo."

"I doubt it, but I'll check. Jesus Paul, you're giving us heart attacks up here. When are you coming back?"

"Probably tomorrow. But call me ASAP about the extradition question."

"Gotcha."

Paul called the airlines, and learned that he could make the trip to Traverse City starting tomorrow morning. Back in the cockpit, he spoke to Juanita and Luis.

"I can't fly until tomorrow. Can I sleep aboard tonight?"

"Of course, my friend," said Luis.

"Here are the keys to the car. It's the red Ford Focus right next to the restaurant. It is rented for a week. You can return it for me next week."

"That is kind of you."

"The least I can do for what you have done for me."

Paul's phone rang. "Yes? Hi Craig. No extradition to Isla Colombo? Thanks buddy."

He gave the thumbs up sign to Juanita and Luis.

Epilogue

It was a fine October afternoon on the calm water near the mouth of the Platte River just north of Point Betsey on Lake Michigan at the western foot of the Leelanau Peninsula, bathed in sunlight and graced by the brilliant fall foliage along the shore. Paul and Joan were in the cockpit of the institute's 35 footer, *Chinook*, fishing for Coho salmon as they had done each fall since two years ago. Paul was helping Joan collect the fish for her dissertation research, and this would provide material for her final set of experiments before finishing her Ph.D. They each held heavy-duty sport fishing rods and were casting bright spinner lures into the clear blue water. A cooler filled with ice sat at the transom, and it already contained three large Cohos.

Joan sat in a deck chair, while her walker was stowed over against the bulkhead behind her. She was able to walk now, but only with heavy dependence on that walker.

"This is heavenly, as always," said Joan.

"Yes, life is good these days," replied Paul.

"Whitetail Lake is recovering pretty well now, I hear."

"Yes, and so is the Boardman River. *Cladophora* mats have been absent now for at least three weeks or so. Things got back to normal for the Traverse City tourist trade well before the end of the season."

"What about Jerry Fenner?"

"He pled guilty to accessory to murder and got fifteen years. He's in Jackson Prison."

"Too bad with Griffin dead there is no way to find out why he was such a misanthropist, and especially a misogynist."

"Well, the last time I saw him I mentioned his mother in a question along those lines, and he exploded in anger. Probably something there. We'll never know."

"And what about your friends Juanita and Luis down in St. Thomas? Do they still have to worry about the charges against them in Isla Colombo? And you too for that matter?"

"No they, or rather we, don't. I just learned from Juanita that they have dropped all charges. Apparently Dr. Mendoza, in whose lab Griffin did his transgenic work, convinced the government there to let it all go. He didn't want continued bad publicity for his lab and for the med school. He actually admitted to what Griffin had done, insisting that Griffin's criminal use of the lethal jellyfish had been kept secret from him, and that my actions and those of Juanita and Luis had been justified. In fact, Juanita and Luis have been invited back to Isla Colombo to resume their lives and careers there. Luis is considering it, because he is having a hard time competing with all of the fishing charters in St. Thomas, but Juanita is very happy in St. Thomas with a permanent job now at an urgent care center."

"That is great news. I hope to meet them someday," said Joan.

"Well, we should go down there this winter and accomplish that."

"I'm in for that!"

They fished in silence for a while, and then Paul's phone rang.

"Hello."

"Paul, this is Juanita."

"Hey, we were just talking about you. How are you?"

"I'm very well thank you. And I have wonderful news. I am engaged to be married!"

"Excellent! To whom?"

"A young doctor at my clinic. Will you come to my wedding?"

"Of course. When is it?"

"February 8th."

"Can I bring a date?"

"Of course. Joan right? What is her last name again?"

"Brockton."

"Oh yes. You will get invitations."

"Thanks Juanita. You too. Bye."

Paul grinned at Joan. "Juanita is getting married in February. We're going."

"Great."

They fished in silence for a while longer. Paul broke the silence.

"Joan, what do you say I call Juanita back and see if she could make it a double wedding?"

Joan stared at the shoreline with very wide eyes. She finally spoke.

"Are you asking me to marry you, Paul Tyson?"

"That I am, sweetie pie."

"Damaged damsel that I am?"

"You're no damsel. You're a formidable scientist, and one hell of a courageous babe. Damaged? Less and less these days."

"But maybe never completely well," Joan said in all seriousness.

"If so, so be it."

Joan rose from her chair, staggered over to Paul and hugged him hard. "Call her."

The afternoon of February 8th was perfect for a beach wedding at Bolongo Bay, St. Thomas. A sun-sparkled light surf washed at the shore of the wide white sand beach, and a moderate wind rustled the palm fronds all around the wedding party. Everyone was dressed in white, some in silk, others in fine linen, and everyone was barefoot. Paul's father sat next to Joan's mother in the front row. Aunts, uncles and cousins of Juanita and Luis were in the front rows as well. Luis had just walked Juanita up the sandy aisle to the flowered arch that graced the beach, and Juanita stood beside her fiancé along with Paul and his best man, Craig Basham. All of them were facing back down the aisle.

Joan stood gripping her walker beside her father as they prepared to come up the aisle.

"Are you ready to surprise Paul, Dad?"

"Ready when you are, big girl."

Joan picked up the walker and threw it to one side. She put her hand lightly on her dad's arm and strode strongly and confidently up the aisle with him. Paul's jaw dropped, and by the time Joan and her dad were halfway to him he was so misted up he could not see the mascara-laden tears streaming down past Joan's wide beaming smile.

AUTHOR'S NOTE

The characters in this story are all fictitious. The Grand Traverse area of Michigan is depicted accurately, with the following exceptions: The limnology institute and university in this story are fictitious, and although I set their location in the approximate area actually occupied by the Great Lakes Campus of Northwestern Michigan College, including the Great Lakes Maritime Academy and the Great Lakes Water Studies Institute, I have never been affiliated with those institutions and have not used them as models for my story in any way. Also, Whitetail Lake is fictitious, although there are numerous lakes like it in the area of its setting.

The Virgin Islands are depicted accurately, except that I fictitiously added the "Spanish Virgin" Isla Colombo and its medical school. The biology and toxicology of the jellyfish, and the biotechnology of gene transfer, are real.

As described in my first novel, *Halcyon Fury*, the book's research vessel *Halcyon* is a fictitious sister ship of a converted wooden minelayer operated in the 1960s and 70s by the University of Michigan as RV *Inland Seas*. Some of the dialog and action on the ship are composites of things that I heard, saw, or did as a student research technician while I was working aboard the *Inland Seas* on Lake Michigan.

Many thanks are due to my "editorial team", Linda Lawler, Barbara Locke, John Locke, Linda Hohm and Chuck Hohm. Any remaining errors in the book are solely my responsibility. During the writing of this book I have continued to benefit from advice that was given me by my friend, author Mary Sanders Smith, while I was writing

Halcyon Fury. Thanks also to my daughter-in-law, Vicki, for the cover photo and my author photo.

Finally, I thank my wife and "chief editor", Lynn, for her love, support and companionship throughout my professional career and for her encouragement of my new adventures into fiction writing.